The Dragon of Emerhill

AN ILLUSTRATED NOVEL

The Dragon of Emerhill

AN ILLUSTRATED NOVEL

WRITTEN AND ILLUSTRATED BY
BRETON W. KAISER TAYLOR

WISHING WILLOW PRESS, CORTE MADERA

The Dragon of Emerhill

Wishing Willow Press / Published by arrangement with Book Passage

This is a fantasy novel. No character names or events refer to anyone living or deceased. Some places are based on European geography. The names Fay Linn and Emerhill are derived from the author's imagination.

ISBN: 978-1-7323269-5-8

Cover and other illustrations © by Breton Kaiser-Shinn
Book design by Jim Shubin, Bookalchemist.net

Edited by Andrea Alban, A.E. Conran, Pamela Feinsilber,
 Sue Heinemann, Anne D. Kaiser Taylor, Amy Novesky,
and Wendy VanHatten.

To William F Kaiser III *in memoriam*
To Shirley Gilbertson, Anne D Kaiser, Robert P. Taylor

And, to my godmother, Pam Kramlich, whose
creativity enhances everything she touches.

Emerhill, a bygone glory;
Kingdom of an age.
Follow here to learn the story
Of a dragon sage.

And a princess, with a father,
Monarch in a rage.
Daughter caught within the stir
Of a battle's stage.

In a rocky cave beneath them,
Hiding for his life,
Dwelled a stout and gentle dragon,
Thought the cause of strife.

What became of royal sailors
Drowned in the sea?
Then, the dragon to the jailer,
Locked up with a key.

Who can say what may have happened,
On that stormy night?
Did the princess or her father
Ever end their fight?

PROLOGUE
The Castle of Lore

Whenever the wind howled Princess Noreia's father would tell her a story.

"The dragons are flying!"he'd say with wide eyes as he dried her tears. "At night, they guard and protect the fairies. Shall I tell you the legend?"

"*Oui*, Papa! *Encore!*"

"*Yes, again?* I will if I can remember...."

"Once a young wizard named Sulien married a sorceress called Acanthia,"he told her, "to unite the human tribes of the vast Lore Kingdom. They built a fine castle and ruled Lore together. They had four children: Enitan, Xiang, Holocene, and their only daughter, Gwenaelle. They lived in a peaceful world, where their dreams came true."

"What did they dream, then, papa? And what did they dream up?"the princess would ask.

"The children went to sleep each night dreaming of magical beings,"Noreia's father would continue. "They awakened to find them before their eyes. When they grew up, they chose to live among the beings of their dreams.

Enitan was the best storyteller. He shared his dreams of castles reaching to the sky, of bridges spanning the outstretched sea. He imagined countries as vast as the oceans, and of peace among the lands.

Gwenaelle dreamed of gentle, winged fairies living in a castle on Lismoire Island, near the coast of Lore.

Xiang dreamed of powerful, majestic dragons on Dragonera Island.

Holocene dreamed of magical birds with magnificent plumage that sang beautiful songs. They lived on the island of Fay Linn.

However, King Sulien yearned for an adventure with his children. One day, when the wind roared in the Kingdom of Lore, he decided to sail away with them. Queen Acanthia protested, of course, but he had made up his mind.

"I beg you not to leave, Sulien. I can't live here alone!"she cried.

"I must find new lands. I long for an adventure!"said the wizard.

Sorceress Acanthia felt abandoned. Then she became angry. Seeking revenge, she circled her wand, leaving her eldest son, Xiang, transformed into a dragon and struggling to escape from her. The king became furious. He released Xiang, who flew away.

The wizard grabbed the wand from his wife, saving the rest of his children. Enitan and Gwenaelle escaped to their father's ship. Holocene ran to reach the others, but Acanthia stopped him at the dock. In his haste, Sulien assumed Holocene was on the ship, and the voyagers set sail.

Wanting to claim her own power, Acanthia turned

Holocene into a seabird and demanded he make her ruler of Fay Linn Kingdom one day.

As for the other children, Prince Xiang joined the dragons and remained with them until the end of his days. Prince Enitan married a fairy.

"A hundred years later,"Noreia's father would conclude, "Gwenaelle married King Aldric of Emerhill. The Castle of Emerhill was built over the ruins of Lore. Then King Aldric died, leaving Queen Gwenaelle to rule until her daughter, Princess Ceana, could take the throne. Then, her daughter Ceana married Prince Roparz ..."

"That's you, Papa!"

"*Oui, ma petite.* I am King Roparz now, married to Queen Ceana, and you and Dalwyn and Argantael are our children!"

After the story, Noreia's father would blow out the candle in the golden candlestick beside her bed, tiptoe out, and close the door.

CHAPTER 1

Gathering Tales

A gust of sea air swept through Noreia's hair, and the open window rattled in the May breeze. A memory flooded her mind, of her young father at her bedside, telling her of flying dragons. Tomorrow was her birthday!

Beyond the royal stables and the Queen Mother's enclosed garden, a dirt path descended from hundred foot high chalky cliffs to the beach below. The old dock and pilings looked tiny from the palace window. Far below Emerhill Castle, waves surged against the cliffs, and the golden ocean stretched out beneath the sun.

The princes's eyes welled with tears as she peered through the leaded glass. With a single gesture, she brushed them away. In the distance, fishermen carried wooden caskets over the sand, followed by a cluster of women in dark cloaks. Nearby, people surrounded a large fishing craft to lay flowers on the bow. Its sails were torn, the rails splintered and broken. Wind blew the whitecaps upon the waves as the gulls scattered from the harbor.

Just as the mourners turned back to the village path, trumpets blared, Noreia stepped back from the window as her parents, King Roparz and Queen Ceana, entered the dining hall. A royal advisor hurried behind them.

"But Your Majesty, we have interviewed the scouts you sent. They reported to have found only one survivor of the royal merchant shipwreck," he told them.

"I will interview him myself, at the royal council this afternoon!" said the king, dismissing the advisor with the back of his hand.

"Roparz, you promised me you would keep us out of war," said Queen Ceana.

"We have lost so many lives thus far. It's my duty to prevent any more," the king told her. He strode over to the window beside Noreia, pulled back the curtain, and surveyed the beach.

"Noreia, come and eat your food." said her mother. Noreia quickly took her seat at the middle of the banquet table, opposite her brother Argantael. Candelabras, platters of smoked mackerel, and trays of sweet crepes adorned the table.

She didn't dare to breathe or move. She and her brothers waited for their father to come away from the window and sit at the head of the table, but he remained lost in thought. The queen walked over to him.

"Do eat your food, dear. You have not slept or eaten!" A woman of beauty, she gently placed her hand in her husband's.

"When the storm raged last night," said Prince Dalwyn, Noreia's older brother, in his usual place at the king's right, "the dragons hid behind the clouds until they emerged to attack the merchant ship, only a few miles from shore. Noreia was out yesterday. She might have been caught in the storm!"

Noreia dropped her fork onto her plate. Now her father knew she had been on the shore. She threw a stinging glance at Dalwyn, who gave her a smirk. He wore his gold and black velvet doublet in the latest style of the Spanish court.

The king's brow tightened. His white bearded jaw clenched as he walked to the head of the long table to sit on his throne. "It's true that the shipwreck last night was caused by a vicious dragon."

"No!" Noreia yelled, dropping her spoon.

"What in the world are you saying?" asked the queen. "Why did you yell at my table?" Noreia's mother dabbed the corners of her mouth with a napkin.

The princess avoided her mother's eyes. "Sorry." Her

head tilted forward. No one knew about the place, past the castle gate and beyond the cliffs, where she could run through the bubbling water without her shoes.

"She always gets dramatic like this," said Argantael. The youngest of the family, he sat quietly across from his sister, his plate piled high with strawberry crepes. He was a thin boy who wore his threadbare velvet cape even at breakfast. His hair was rarely combed.

"Father, I'm prepared to defend Emerhill against the dragons," Dalwyn said. "I'm the best in my fencing class!" He was a debonair boy of eighteen, with wavy hair like Noreia's, but that is where their similarities ended.

"Dalwyn, why do you have to bring up fighting now?" Noreia asked.

"Noreia, please!" said her mother. "Eat your breakfast."

"And Father says I can get a new broadsword, didn't you, Father?"

"Dalwyn, this is not a game! Emerhill village has lost a hundred lives. We are not playing with toy soldiers, boy! Sailors died in the shipwreck caused by a malicious dragon."

"That's not true!" cried Noreia. "It was the storm, Father, off the coast of our kingdom. The ship was wrecked in the storm. The dragons wouldn't attack a ship flying our flag."

"Enough!" said her father, stabbing a piece of mackerel. An awkward silence followed.

"Dalwyn, place your napkin in your lap, not in your collar," said Gwenaelle, the elderly Queen Mother, her white hair held back by a wimple. She gestured to a servant at the edge of the room. "Would someone else care for more poached eggs? Duana makes the best eggs Provençal in the world."

A footman with shaking hands brought the poached egg tray to each of the six family members in turn.

"Ceana, I have no choice. We must do something about the dragons!" said the king. "I've organized a council with my infantry this afternoon to discuss the problem. The villagers and noblemen will be here to voice their complaints."

"Dear, try to negotiate a way to avoid bloodshed. Wars are costly and lead to misery for so many," said the queen.

"Yes, I'll do my best, Ceana."

"Father, are you sure the dragons are the enemy?" Noreia dared to ask.

"Of course they are!" said the king. "They cause ships to sink with their valuable goods. We have many fishermen and sailors who have never returned to these shores. Dragons are destructive, my daughter, and cruel!"

"But you told me they were harmless when I was little.... It was the storm, Father. The dragons didn't—"

"Don't talk back to your father, Noreia," interrupted the queen. "I expect better from you. Why must you be so willful?"

"I am not being willful," Noreia said softly.

"What's that you're mumbling?" her father asked, leaning forward.

"Nothing, sir."

"Noreia, a dragon was seen flying directly overhead when

the Emerhill merchant ship was brutally attacked." The king pounded his fist on the table.

"Listen to your father."

"They're ferocious reptiles. They have awful scales and measure twice the size of an elephant!" Dalwyn added.

"That's not true! Dragons are mammals. They are warm blooded like us," said Noreia.

"Neither one of you is right," Prince Argantael told them. "Dragons are neither reptiles nor mammals. Like mammals, they're warm blooded. However, they have the scales of a reptile. Dragons breathe fire because their vascular system draws heat from the sun. They remain unclassified to this day. In fact, I've read—"

"Quiet, Argantael! You've exhausted the subject."

"Sorry, Father. But what happened to the dragon..." Noreia paused as the king glowered,

"...the, um, *ferocious* dragon who attacked the ship?" She looked up at her father.

"In the middle of the storm, the captain ordered his crew to fire in the direction the dragon was flying away. An excellent bowman shot it," said the king.

Noreia jumped from her chair. "But they are innocent, Father—"

"Quiet, Noreia!"

"Sorry, sir. May I be excused, Mother?"

"Yes, dear, if you are finished," said her mother with a deep hearted sigh.

"Noreia?" The girl stopped short and turned to face the Queen Mother, whose velvet sleeves, she noticed, were moist with peat moss.

"Yes, Grandmother Gwenaelle?"

"If you are going into the garden, please bring back some French lavender for your mother's sachet. The scent relaxes her. And Duana wants some rosemary to use in preparing dinner tonight." The old woman took a bite of bread with blackberry preserves. "Are you looking forward to your birthday? Your dear friend Lisette is coming to stay. You will have a chance to visit with her parents, Fairy Queen Perizada and King Arne. Green linens and a bouquet of fuchsias and jasmine, or maybe—"

"Mother, we don't need to talk about this now!" said the king.

"Now, Roparz, you must watch your temper, dear. You haven't touched your asparagus," said Queen Gwenaelle.

"Don't fuss over me, Mother!" The king threw down his napkin like a gauntlet.

"Dear, will you pass me the—" said the elderly queen. "That's it!" The king jumped to his feet. "I swear I have got to do something about those dragons!"

Noreia rushed out of the room.

"Come back here, young lady!" called her father.

"Let her go, dear. You know how she is," said Queen Ceana.

CHAPTER 2
Questioning the Enemy

To avoid the guards, Noreia would need to take an alternate route to leave the house. She slipped through the door under the staircase, down a stairway, and out into the courtyard. Rising from its slumber, the sun was gentle and warm. Cascades of flowering vines draped themselves through the trellis above her. A topiary artist was busy shaping the boxwood, and a fountain gurgled near the terrace.

The princess yearned to stop there, because the garden promised her such peacefulness. Thinking of her journey again, she ran through a colonnade, where statues of fairies stood in heroic poses on pedestals. These were people of her favorite legends, poems, and books—Queen Perizada and her fairy daughters and the heroic young Xiang, the boy turned into a dragon by Acanthia, the sorceress.

Onward she ran, past stone columns with their gargoyle capitals and carvings. As she rushed through her grandmother's flower garden, she grabbed tufts of lavender and sprigs of rosemary and tucked them into her belt.

Slipping back inside, she crept through the marble floored war room, with its cases of ornate swords from heroic battles, and its giant globe mounted on a walnut stand. The back wall was speckled with Greek tesserae, the tiles creating a map of Brittany and the surrounding islands.

She quickened her stride through the throne room, with its imposing gold leaf thrones.

Noreia went through the door into the kitchen wing. "*Pardonez-moi*," she said. *Excuse me!* Light fell onto a baking table cluttered with sackcloth bags of millet flour. The head cook, Duana, turned to Noreia as she swept by. The Princess ran past the cook's assistant, who was stamping out leaves of dough on the powdery marble. They were making pheasant pies. Fresh farm eggs in wicker baskets crowded a table near the bakers.

"Watch where you step, child," said Duana as she stirred a pot of soup. "Such a sad face. Your Highness, what's gotten into you? Have you brought the rosemary for the pie, my dear?" Noreia pulled a bundle of rosemary from her pocket. "*Merci, ma petite!* " Noreia's nickname was *my little one.*

Noreia tiptoed through the crowded pantry, filled with people and hanging clusters of dried flowers. She stepped into the fenced yard, where the geese honked and the hens cackled. She lifted the latch on the wooden gate, all the while holding her breath, but it opened without a squeak. When she reached the walkway, she took off her brocade slippers and stuffed them under a loose slab of flagstone.

As she looked out onto the Atlantic, Noreia's face caught the morning sun. Emerhill Castle commanded a view above merchant galleons and fishing craft. Noreia breathed in the briny scent of mackerel and sardines, and the carefree smell of the sea. Below her, the harbor was a forest of masts with laddered rigging and gathered sails. Out on the water, the ships' hulls smacked against the rollicking waves.

She ran on until she reached a stone bridge that stretched over a ravine. Her father had told her that it was built in the days of the Romans. He'd said that if it had lasted this long, it would never collapse, but she never felt safe on it.

She nearly lost her footing on the cobblestones. She thought of her father's words as she crossed the bridge, never daring to look down.

Noreia, now barefoot, stepped down from the cliff and took the dirt path to the harbor. The path switched back and forth as she descended the rocky stairs. Rushing forward, she felt a cramp in her side. She caught her breath.

"What if I can do nothing to change Father's mind?" she whispered over the sound of the wind. "I've got to try." With careful scrutiny, Noreia surveyed the way the path wound down to the sea.

She ran down the path, toward the treacherous craggy cliffs looming over the sea, her heart racing. Once on the beach, she would know the way, if only she could get there in time. She climbed onto a giant boulder overlooking the sea and glimpsed the sparkling water, stretching out beneath the sun.

When she reached the far end of the sand, the beach was crowded with ice plants and pulpy kelp that had washed ashore.

Just a week ago, Noreia brought seaweed to a dragon called Stalwart, who had found shelter in a sea cave below the castle. She had first spotted him while climbing the hillside to look at the blue painted boats in the harbor. When she got to him, he was lying unconscious from a head wound.

She hopped nimbly over the rocks. She thought back to the bandage she had made from her apron, and the blood on her hands. Now, hovering in her mind was the thought that Stalwart might be the dragon who was shot by one of her father's men. She stared back at her father's castle, perched at the top of a chalky cliff. Its austere towers stood firm despite the storm, the desperate villagers, and her wounded friend. She pressed on into the wind, over the rocks, until she reached Stalwart's cave.

She climbed inside his limestone shelter, carved out by saltwater after thousands of years of wear. Water dripped from the roof of the cave into a lagoon within the walls of quiet stone. A small river ran between the boulders and the pointed stalagmites that pushed up from the floor.

Noreia found Stalwart hiding behind the waterfall in an underground cavern. The dragon seemed larger than she remembered. A bright, narrow shaft of sunlight lit his shimmering dark blue scales like the ocean at night. His strong limbs were heavy with muscles. Weary, aged eyes looked up at her.

"Stalwart! Are you all right?" called Noreia. Her voice echoed loudly. Stalwart's rumbling voice shook the ground.

"I know they hurt you! I'm sorry, Stalwart." Noreia trod softly through the sacred space.

"Do not be sorry, Princess. You are not like them at all!" said Dormach.

"No, you don't understand. They are good people, Stalwart. They are afraid, though. My father—"

"Your father's sailors struck me with that arrow!" The

dragon eased closer to her, around the waterfall, and his great teeth shone as he spoke. His huge eyes inspected her face for a reaction.

"I know, Stalwart. Father said one of his archers hit a dragon," Noreia said.

"Last night, I tested my wings here, beside the shore of Brittany, seeking giant sea kelp to eat. I spotted a canopy of sea kelp on the surface of the waves. I dove down into the water, finding myself in a dense forest of long, leafy strands. They were healthy and rich in minerals. After I had torn away a strand in my teeth, I resurfaced.

There was a ship of scrambling sailors and yelling voices. Like a dagger, something sharp and painful pierced me," Stalwart moaned. "Clouds of blood billowed throughout the underwater kelp forest. The curve of a gigantic ship swept by me."

"The captain gave the order to one of his men to shoot. It should never have happened," said Noreia.

There was a rumbling as the dragon shifted his weight to show her his wound. "Here, under my wing. It hurts more today than yesterday."

"It's a clean wound, though, due to the saltwater," said Noreia. "I'm hopeful you'll feel better soon."

Then there was silence, except for the flow of the waterfall.

"Roparz, the king...my father...has ordered a council meeting today to determine a course of action."

"And you, Noreia, what will you do?" asked the dragon softly.

"I will think of a plan. My father doesn't know you are here, but he knows I was on the beach before the storm. When I ran to your cave for cover, the rain came down, echoing in these walls, remember? Flashes of light lit the dark sky and surrounding stone like the fleeting moon before she disappears behind a cloud. And then you told *me* not to be afraid."

And now there was a silence that Noreia could not endure. "Aren't you afraid, Stalwart? They could kill you!"

"Noreia, I am three hundred years old. Dragons once governed the Realm of the Sea. It is time for a new guardian of the Sea Realm. I can defend myself against a few fishermen."

"No—please listen to reason, my friend!"

"It's dangerous for you to stay. Go back to your father, Princess." The dragon curled back into his corner.

"No, Stalwart. I don't think that way," said Noreia. " You are my friend! I 'll stand by you. I wish you could fly to a safe place, far away from here," she said.

"When will you have enough strength to fly?"

"In two days, I'll be healed enough to fly home to Dragonera Island, the home of my ancestors."

"And today I will discover my father's plan, when I listen in at the council meeting. I'll help you escape. Maybe you can take me to your island.

"To an island of dragons, Princess? Isn't your place here, with your family?"

"Stalwart, I...I'll meet you under the bridge in a few hours. I'll tell you what father has decided."

"I think I can be there, Princess, when the village clock chimes two."

The sun was brilliant as Princess Noreia crawled out from the darkness. An awkward cry of seabirds startled her as the noon church bell tolled.

The King's Council! Noreia forced herself to start the climb back up to the castle. She trained her eyes on the path before her, praying she would arrive in time to overhear the council's plans.

CHAPTER 3

Spying on Warriors

Nearing the castle, Noreia climbed to a precipice over-looking the sea. A kitchen maid was walking toward her from the fishing boats, carrying a bucket of mackerel. She waved to Noreia to accompany her the rest of the way home.

"Princess Noreia! Please hurry, Your Highness. Your grandmother needs the herbs she requested right away," said the maid, putting down the heavy bucket for a moment.

The princess let out a deep breath. "Yes, but why are you in such a hurry?" Noreia asked, catching her breath.

"I...I'll hear from Her Majesty about this if you are late for the council luncheon!" the red headed woman replied, wiping the sweat from her brow.

"Marie, have the villagers and knights arrived for the council?"

"No, Your Highness. Not yet."

As the princess followed the woman over the stone bridge, she noticed a group of peasants heading to the castle gate and a cluster of nobles and other courtiers talking on the terrace. The king would be granting them an audience soon.

They walked under a rose trellis and stumbled along the cobblestone path. Noreia unlatched the creaky gate and grabbed her shoes from under the flagstone.

The maid lugged the bucket into the yard. Noreia elbowed the Dutch door to the kitchen ajar.

"There you are!" cried Duana. "Hurry, Noreia. When will you start being an obedient girl? Comb your hair, and don't go barefoot to climb the cliffs again." Duana smoothed the princess' loose forelock into a hair ribbon she brought from her pocket.

Noreia kissed Duana on both cheeks and then rushed by her, past an assistant chef stacking yellow glazed plates for the luncheon table. Pushing through the crowd of bakers, Noreia collided with a kitchen girl carrying a basket of eggs. As the basket fell through the air, the cooks stood like garden statues, and an astonished Duana stopped her work.

"Forgive me!" The teenage girl began picking the broken eggshells off the floor.

"It was my fault, I bumped into you." Noreia leaned down to help the girl, but a butler ushered her away into a corridor.

The service hall was cluttered with people. Two men passed by with trays of glinting goblets and entered the dining hall balancing the stemware. The princess retreated to a dark corner of the corridor. She could hear the silverware and platters chiming from the dining room, where the councilmen would assemble for the luncheon.

A beam of light led her to an old knothole in the wall, which she and Argantael had once used to spy on the royal guests. Kneeling down, she looked into the grand throne room and at the two gilded thrones on a wide raised marble platform. The light of midday poured from clerestory windows onto the glossy French oak cabinets and Italian walnut chairs. On one wall hung an elaborate tapestry with a fire breathing dragon and the Emerhill coat of arms.

Golden light fell upon the king's profile as his servant pulled aside the heavy window curtains. He was a strong man, wearing a long green tunic over his shimmering armor, a velvet cape fastened to his shoulder. He handed a sheathed sword to his royal page. When the queen entered in a long, belted bliaut and a circlet of silver, a hand maiden accepted her long cloak. Two young servants carried in a wooden stand and set it beside the marble steps before the throne. A fine wooden chair was brought in for the witness stand, followed by four chairs for the Noblemen's Council.

Colorful pennants with tricolored emblems in olive-green, goldenrod, and teal blue satin hung above the gathered crowd. At the front of the crowd were the foppish courtiers and stern landholders. Silversmiths, street peddlers, barkeepers, and stonemasons stood toward the back of the room. Tanners and blacksmiths, rope makers, shipwrights, and weavers had all managed to fit into the grand throne room. Their animated discussions fascinated Noreia.

The king cleared his throat. "My fellow council members! The dragons have threatened our harbor and endangered the people of Emerhill! The reason I have called this council is to find out exactly what happened to our merchant ship last night. We shall also discover how the fishing boat sank!" Her father's voice resounded through the rafters.

Princess Noreia released a long, shaky breath. She made her breathing calm and her movements still.

Her father slammed his fist onto the arm of his throne. "This dragon's attack is a tragedy for our kingdom. Emerhill Kingdom must be strong to face its enemies. We will hear both sides of this case, however, so that justice shall prevail."

The princess steadied her position in her hiding place, conscious of the creaky floorboards beneath her. A royal waiter hurried past with a weighty terrine of pheasant pie.

"Excuse me, Your Highness," he said, stepping around Noreia.

She looked back into the grand throne room as the king's servant, a boy her own age, presented His Majesty with his crown and scepter. Another young man handed him a letter, which His Majesty tore through in a second.

"Yes, yes," he said, reading the letter. "Well, then. Thank you, boy! You may go." He stood again to address the crowd. "I have just received a report of the number of deaths from the shipwreck last night. It is not only an unfortunate number. It is tragic."

"The fishermen and sailors have begun calling this disaster *the Great Storm*, and I agree that the event should be remembered. We shall henceforth commemorate yesterday as the Day of the Great Storm. There will be an appropriate funeral for those who died hence. Thank you!"

A silence fell upon the crowd as all waited for any pearl of wisdom that His Majesty might add.

Argantael sat by the window, immersed in his leather-bound book. For a moment, his eyes traveled over to his father, then to the knights. The boy buried his face in his book again, his eyes trained upon his reading.

The king's heavy shoes rattled as he paced the throne room. His cavalrymen, holding their plumed helmets, entered the room and stood in groups at the back of the crowd. Then the king cleared his throat.

"Call the first witness in defense of the kingdom! Silence! Please," said the king. "The first witness is the sole survivor of the sunken merchant ship. He claims to have seen the dragon. Step forward, man!" The sailor stood as straight as he could. "I thank you for your trouble, sailor. Can you describe what you experienced during the shipwreck?"

"I was on the lower deck when the storm picked up, Your Majesty," the sailor began.

"Did you know there would be a storm?"

"Yes, there had been a red sky at dawn, Your Majesty," said the sailor.

"Very well. Continue," said the king.

"The storm started as heavy rainfall. The west wind enveloped the sails as the rain came down in sheets. High-crested waves smacked against the sides of the boat. Our boat tipped at a dangerous angle, until many of us slid across the deck. Some of the men were bruised or unconscious. Then, out of nowhere, came a fanged dragon as thirsty as a tiger, and taller than a masthead. His eyes were like flames, looking down at me like the beast he was. That's how I know it was the dragon for sure!"

"So do you believe the dragon attacked your ship?" asked the king.

"It was as I have said, Your Majesty! He was there, before my own eyes. The wicked beast wanted to—"

"Did you see the dragon strike the ship?" asked the king.

"The wind and the water knocked me onto the deck. The dragon slipped away from me. I know he sank the ship, though," the sailor replied.

"Thank you. The witness may be excused from court." The sailor left the room.

"Second witness, please. Bring in the fisherman!" ordered the king. An old seafarer was brought forward to testify.

"What happened last night, from your recollections of the storm?" His Majesty asked the witness.

"Our boat was nearby when the dragon flew toward the ship. Frightful!" said the gaunt fisherman.

"Did you see the dragon attack the ship with the Emerhill flag? Think carefully," said the king.

"I saw the dragon as big as life before me. Your Majesty, I saw it hover over the boat like a horrible bat. It rode the wind through the clouds and dove into the water, making tremendous waves that shook our fishing boat! I'm sure that dragon sank the ship!"

The queen reached over and placed a hand upon her husband's arm. "May I speak with you in private, Roparz?" she whispered. The king and queen stood and went to a quiet corner, away from the crowd. Noreia overheard them, from her knot hole, near a hanging tapestry. "Alas, my dearest husband. Are you sure about this? How do you know that the dragon in question was not flying by, without any intent to harm the ships?" asked the queen, still whispering.

"Ceana, I—"

"No, my husband. Just remember the stories of your ancestors. Many magical beings look to the dragons for help," the queen said.

"I have witnesses, Ceana. Evidence!"

"Certainly. But if you lead Emerhill into war, remember the ruin on which this castle stands. The Castle of Lore, Roparz," she reminded him. "The dragons are a part of us, too."

The crowd was uneasy as King Roparz returned to his throne and thought for a moment.

"Excellent," he told the fisherman. " We thank you for your testimony on behalf of the kingdom!" The fisherman bowed low and exited.

The king paced the floor and then spoke. "In this case, we would assume guilt on the part of the dragon ...except...except...we must examine the proximity of the dragon to the boat. A witness may have seen the dragon from the castle. Sir Alwyn, you may testify!"

As the noblemen gathered around great clustered columns of stone, they clung to his words. The soldiers' voices overlapped in discussion.

"Order, please!" shouted the king.

The king turned toward a window to survey the outside main court, enclosed by a stone curtain wall and guarded towers. Then he turned back to face the crowd.

"Gentlemen, please! One at a time!" said King Roparz. "Sir Alwyn may speak. Step forward and let us hear your account of what happened last night."

CHAPTER 4
The Emerhill Council

"I do recall the storm, Your Majesty. I regret that I honestly couldn't see the dragon attack the ship from where I stood, because the rain was so heavy," said Sir Alwyn. A portly man in a sensible brown doublet, wearing a fine ruff collar and a velvet hat, he possessed the elegance of a nobleman.

"Where were you standing exactly, Your Lordship?" asked the king.

Sir Alwyn stroked his beard, lost in thought. "The southwestern tower atop the main gate, facing the Atlantic. I had plans to travel that evening, Your Majesty," said the knight. "I changed my mind due to the gathering storm. It was the worst storm we've had in many a year. And in the early spring, no less!"

"Then we must conclude that our decision depends upon—" The king caught a look from the queen and paused. "Now we must look into the condition of the ship. I call the head carpenter to the stand!"

Carrying a wooden toolbox, the lanky head carpenter found his way through the crowd and quietly took the stand.

"Did you examine the ship prior to its leaving?"

"I did, as Your Majesty requires," said the carpenter.

"What did you find?"

There was a problem with some of the floorboards, which needed to be replaced," the carpenter remembered.

"Why?" asked the king.

"There was dry rot in them, and some were splintered."

"Might this damage have caused a ship to sink?" asked the king, stroking *his* beard.

"I think the ship was in fine condition otherwise, Your Majesty!"

"Answer the question, please. Could it have been in danger in the middle of a storm?"

"It might have, yes. But it was in good condition. I would never have let the boat out of dry dock if I'd thought...." The carpenter shifted in his chair.

"Enough." King Roparz leaned his head against the back of the throne, rubbed his brow, and closed his eyes. Then he leaned forward, resting his hands on his sword due to a shoulder wound. "We don't have enough certain and substantial evidence that the dragon in question had intent to sink, or indeed sank, the two ships."

"But Sire, our villagers must have protection!" cried a village merchant. "Emerhill itself could be attacked!"

"Our ships are in danger, too!" shouted a fisherman.

King Roparz leaned his hand upon the arm of his throne.

"I'll join the fight!" said a farmer, holding a rake aloft.

A woman pushed her way to the front of the gathering. She wore the spectacles and graying hair of one who had finished raising a family. Her modest dress was one of a merchant's wife.

"My husband lies dead because of this dragon. My boy lies dead, too, because of this dreadful beast. The people of Emerhill know that dragons cause storms and sink ships. How much proof is needed before we act?"

"How can the king stay silent when we should be at war with our enemy?" asked the farmer.

"Father, let us not waste any time in mourning what happened, or might happen," said Dalwyn. "We must act swiftly, and we must act now! Follow me, men!"

"Dalwyn, let us not be o'er hasty in our decision," the king told his son. "The storm must be considered in this case."

"Strategy is the first priority now, Father! Avenge the lost sailors! Protect the people of Emerhill. Long live King Roparz!" Dalwyn carried a long sword in an ornate sheath. Now, withdrawing it, he plunged it into the floor and copied the proud stance of his father.

The queen set her embroidery hoop upon the arm of her throne. When Queen Ceana stood, the whole council was quiet. Her distraught face revealed her concern. Turning to the king, she whispered, "Did you think of the risk to your life, husband? Do you have to go to war with the dragons?"

Noreia's father was stern as he whispered back, "Do not worry your head with such matters, Ceana. I will defend our home!"

As the queen and her attendants stepped down from the throne platform, the king made a toast to her.

"The queen swoons when we talk of war!" said Sir Alwyn, lifting his pewter mug.

"To Her Majesty, Queen Ceana!" shouted a knight, raising his pewter mug high.

The soldiers lifted their mugs in turn. "To Her Majesty!"

The assembled knights bowed deeply as the queen led her ladies through the parting crowd. They were like a gentle wind, as their lovely veils floated through the forest of soldiers.

"The dragons will be our target, men. Leave the battle plans to me. Together we will carry the battle to the finish!" said the king.

"If I were to run into a dragon, I'd skewer him like a fish!" Prince Dalwyn raised his sword. The men cheered the young prince, shouting and clanging their mugs together. In the echoing room, they raised their swords to salute their crown prince. He handed his sword to his apprentice and bowed to his father with a punctuated nod.

"Your Majesty, on behalf of all the lords of Emerhill, you have our support," said Sir Frederick, the king's falconer. He was a tall, mysterious man with small eyes that shifted from the king to the bird on his arm and back again. The man adjusted the leather hood covering the bird's head. Then he stepped toward the throne. "That dragon monster would terrify any man," he said, "but the horrible beast was seen near Your Majesty's castle. You may need to send scouts to the surrounding areas to look for more!"

"More? What do you mean, Sir Frederick?" roared the king. "Is he not the last dragon of Emerhill, shot down by our own men?"

"Perhaps, Your Majesty," said Sir Frederick in a low voice. "But recently, dragons were sighted off the coast of Spain. If Your Majesty agrees to lead a hunting voyage to the islands there, we could get rid of the dragons once and for all." A hush fell over the crowd as all waited for the king's response.

"Count me in!" said a nobleman.

"For Emerhill!" shouted a gallant knight.

"We have no need to investigate further. Dragons are ferocious enemies!" The king's deep voice echoed throughout the room. "I want my soldiery to search our coastline for any beasts!"

Noreia cringed at the clamber of pots and pans behind her.

"And then, brave knights, noblemen, and esteemed councilmen, I'll lead you all to the dragon's isle, and by the power of my sword, each dragon shall die!" declared King Roparz.

The men threw their arms around each other, holding up their swords. They leapt to take each other's hands.

The king's eyes flashed with a rage that Noreia had never understood. "Listen, men. Together we shall defeat the breed of monsters. There will not be one dragon left within our realm! The dragons' tyranny will be mere fable!" His voice resonated beyond the throne room.

His soldiers clattered off to their posts. The citizenry and courtiers cheered.

Princess Noreia slowed her breathing again to listen for the fading voices. The soldiers' chatter became echoes. Again, the king cleared his throat.

"Dalwyn, following my death, you will be king. You will rule this land alone. You shall command the fine soldiery I have trained. Leading only the finest, you must destroy every dragon!"

"Yes, Father!"

The princess slid to the cold stone floor of the service hall. She clasped her hand over her mouth and wept. She couldn't believe her father would kill the creatures she had loved since she was a child.

"Do not fail at our mission!" Her father's voice chased away her tears. The princess listened for the vanishing clang of armor as the king and Prince Dalwyn's footsteps receded into the distant hallway.

"No," the princess uttered softly to herself. "If you go to find Stalwart, he will be gone."

CHAPTER 5

A Storm of Cavalry

Noreia's pulse raced with the wind. She had to reach Stalwart's cave before her father's scouts discovered him. If only she didn't have to wear a dress, she could climb the cliffs faster.

Noreia placed her foot against a rock to brace herself. She looked out over the boulders and down at the beach, where the sun shone its brightest. She ran down the dirt path, avoiding the grasses and branches in her way. The church bell in the village struck one.

As Noreia neared Stalwart's cave, she heard a voice rising from below. She turned around as the wind lifted the sound to her from the beach. It was the sound of breathing, or rather, a coarse gruff sound like several lions snoring. Slowly, she crept over the rocks to observe what was taking place.

In horror, she witnessed the great dragon, Stalwart, held captive under a huge fishing net on the shore. Noreia's fingers gripped the rocks. It was too late, and all was lost.

The dragon's strong limbs tensed as he struggled against the ropes, trying to shake off his captors. His proud head shook as he bared his fangs. His teal green eyes reflected the light as he thrashed his barbed tail. Thirteen fishermen and ten of the king's soldiers surrounded him, holding the net. Pulling and grasping, their hands were one combined force. They had not broken him, but the arrow wound was recent and severe enough to cause him to lose strength. They had captured him.

Two elegant rows of knights on horseback rode over the dunes. Their plumed helmets flashed in the sun.

"This one will catch a fine fortune for each of us. We'll be promoted in the ranks as soon as he's in the dungeon. What a life we will have!" shouted the first knight.

"Don't forget that I have first pick of anything the king offers us. It was my idea to search the beach," said the second one. Stalwart gritted his teeth and reared at them like a wild stallion. He roared and snapped at them and clawed the rope net. Stalwart needed Noreia's help, but she couldn't stop the soldiers. She had to rescue him, but how?

She would persuade her mother to speak to her father. He might listen to her mother's words, so calming and wise.

Noreia reached the empty throne room, thinking by chance that she might find her mother. Her mother's throne was empty.

There was a door left open to the columned courtyard. Grandmother Gwenaelle's wisteria vines draped over the window outside the throne room, where Argantael was absorbed in reading a thick volume at the marble exedra.

"Argantael! Have you been reading here this whole time?"

"I'm reading *The History of The Decline and Fall of the Roman Empire*," her brother responded.

"Has it fallen?" Noreia asked.

Argantael looked up for a moment and stared at her through his spectacles. "Not yet. I'm only on page 967."

"Where's Mother?" Noreia panted, trying to slow her breathing.

"She's embroidering in her sitting room. I wouldn't bother her now, Noreia."

"But I need to talk with her!" said Noreia. "Now." Noreia stopped, her hand still on the latch of the French doors that led to the central courtyard.

"Now is not a good time. She is saddened by the loss of the sailors on Father's ship. She knows that he might go to war. We could lose him, Noreia."

"So why are you sitting still, reading?" she asked.

Argantael looked up from the book. "I don't know. This is a good book."

"Where is Grandmother Gwenaelle?"

"She's in the herb garden." Argantael marked his place with a ribbon and put down the book. He stared at the orderly garden through a row of columns.

"What's wrong?" she asked.

Argantael shrugged. His brown eyes looked at her briefly. "Nothing." He turned back to the window. A tiny goldfinch was preening in the maple tree just outside.

"Argantael, I know when you are afraid to tell me what's bothering you."

Argantael turned his head away, trying to hide his tear-streamed face. He wiped his eyes on a shirtsleeve. "All right. Father has invited me to go on the voyage to Dragonera

Island with his army."

"No! Argantael, you mustn't go. You've got to listen to me! Father has captured a dragon, Stalwart, only a few paces from his cave. He's injured and held captive in a net! And they are taking him to the dungeon."

"You're telling me there's a dragon held prisoner here, near this castle?"

"Yes, and I want to set him free. You have to help me," Noreia demanded. "Then, I can fly to Dragonera to warn the dragons on the island of Father's plan. But I need your help, Argantael. You're going to get me into Father's library!"

Argantael held up a firm hand, as if to block her words from racing forward. "Hold on. I am?" he asked. "Why?"

"You're constantly lost in those books of yours!" Noreia snapped. "Once in a while, couldn't you understand me? I need to find out how to survive on that island, so that I can warn the dragons!"

"Why do the dragons matter to you, Noreia?"

"I know one. Stalwart is my friend. I talk with him every day. He is wise and has been kind to me. And I'm not going to stand around and watch Father destroy his family or his home!" Noreia charged out of the doors to her grandmother's garden and hurried through the stone columns caked with moss.

"Noreia, dear, pass me one of those meadowsweet bulbs, please. Your friends Princess Adisa and Princess Ying will be here soon to attend your birthday party." The elderly queen mother was kneeling in front of a muddy flowerbed, in a Burgundian gown with long over sleeves that dragged over the cobblestone pavers.

"Yes, Grandmother! But I need to speak with you!" The princess handed her grandmother a burlap bag from a wooden bucket. Her grandmother dug her fragile hands into the dirt, which she had carved into small squares. Calendula and elecampane bordered every square, each carefully placed to utilize sunlight or shade. Queen Gwenaelle was planting healing herbs for each ailment.

"Noreia, dear. Watch how I placed each of these bulbs. Each one needs the right amount of water and sun. Some need shade. A princess is such a flower, you see. She must have just the right amount of shade and sun. Every herb has its purpose, do you understand? There, now." Noreia's grandmother brushed the soil from her canvas apron.

"I must talk to you, Grandmother Gwenaelle."

"Yes, I know, dear. Our work together will save lives one day. Eventually, this garden will belong to you."

"Yes, thank you. May I ask you a question, please?"

"Please don't interrupt, dear. I'm busy now, anyway," said the queen, stuffing dirt around tiny seeds of lemon balm and meadowsweet. "Meadowsweet and lemon balm are healing. Do you know how nice lavender can be for relaxation, dear?"

"But I have a question I need to ask *you*. May I?" asked the princess, catching her breath. Her grandmother stood up and squinted, and began snipping roses with long stems. Blossoming orange trees and yellow nasturtiums attracted hummingbirds to hover, alight, and hasten away.

"I'm listening, dear," said Queen Gwenaelle, her eyes trained upon a potted lemon tree.

"Grandmother, I don't know what to do about something. Can you help me?"

"Yes, if I can, dear."

"I know someone...who has become a good friend to me. And he's in a lot of trouble. My father has thrown him into the dungeon. What can I do to help him?" Noreia leaned forward, listening carefully.

"I don't meddle in matters of state, Noreia! That wouldn't be ladylike."

"Grandmother, please. It's important. I'm afraid."

"I can tell you a secret, but you mustn't let anyone know that I...." Noreia's grandmother glanced over her shoulder.

"I promise I won't say a word," Noreia vowed.

"A secret way leads to the dungeon from this garden. If you use your knowledge of the garden, you may find the way in." The old woman yawned and sighed, wiping her spectacles.

"Grandmother Gwenaelle, how can I find that place? I'd hoped you might know how I can obtain the dungeon key. Do you remember?" Noreia asked.

"I know a key is hidden in the garden, yes."

"Where?" Noreia hurried alongside her grandmother. "What does that mean, Grandmother?"

"Leave no stone unturned, that's the key," said the queen with a wink. "When the moon shines upon the dungeon key, you will know it is time."

"I won't ever find it in time. Why won't you tell me?"

"As a young queen in this castle, I never dared go to the dungeon. Now you will find it. I have so much faith in you!" Her grandmother took Noreia's hand in hers and held it to her cheek. "My dear granddaughter. Promise me you'll never lose your curiosity, or your hope!"

"Your Majesty!" Nissa, the queen's chambermaid, rushed over with a cloak draped over her arm. "I'm here to get you dressed. His Majesty would dislike you getting dirt on the hem of your fine houppelande again!" Nissa frowned as she guided the queen mother onto the garden path.

"Nissa, wait! It's just that I need to speak to Grandmother about the voyage to—"

"Noreia, I wish your father would spend more time in this garden with me. As a boy, he used to assist me. I'm trying to finish this bed of medicinal herbs. This garden will be yours someday. Yours to tend, and to utilize the plants I've taught you about. Perhaps you can finish the work I began."

"Yes, Grandmother."

Noreia's grandmother shuffled along the path with her chambermaid, toward her own wing of the castle. Her steps were measured and slow.

Irises in crimson and white grew within the boundaries of a wall. Beyond the wall of her grandmother's tended garden was a vast green estate that spilled over the hillsides toward the mountains in the distance. To the northeast was the winding dirt path to the village of Emerhill. To the east, the king's hunting grounds began. The northwest side of the castle led to the royal stables. The southern stretch of wall faced the great Atlantic Sea.

As long as she could remember, Noreia had sensed she was surrounded by magic. The princess was convinced that an ancient mystical civilization could be reached if only she could find the key. Beneath the flickering trellises of her grandmother's garden, a world of light was hidden.

CHAPTER 6

The Arrival of the Carriages

Noreia sighed, watching the sunlight shine through the leaves of the lemon trees. She listened to the fountain trickle in the center of the garden.

The door was open to the music room, where the queen was embroidering and talking with her husband while a minstrel played sweetly on a lute. The queen was crying. "What will I do if you are killed in battle, Roparz? Or, what if you are involved in a shipwreck? The kingdom would be without a leader!" the queen asked.

"Ceana, I must carry out my mission. Emerhill shall be run by Prince Dalwyn until I return, and—"

"Dalwyn is too inexperienced," said Queen Ceana. "He cannot run a kingdom on his own!"

"Ceana, Dalwyn is taking fencing classes each day. He'll be a great general when the time comes."

"Then why does he seem to have his head in the clouds! He talks about waging battle against dragons, but he spends too much time antagonizing poor Noreia. If I were her age, I wouldn't know what to do with him!"

"While I'm gone, we could appoint advisors, and learned men who—"

"Roparz, how sure are you that these dragons are worth so great a cost?" The queen stood her ground. "Many knights and foot soldiers will be killed. How are their families going to be rewarded for their loss?"

"Our brave knights would be proud to fight for Emerhill," the king told her.

"Their families will be honored appropriately."

"Think about me, then. If you go, there's a high probability that you will not return. What guarantee can you give me, my husband, that Emerhill will be safer after this voyage?"

King Roparz turned to meet Ceana's eyes.

Noreia paced around the fountain, pondering what she could do. She twisted a lock of her dark hair with a strong tug. She really wanted to turn and run. She could make an excuse for herself, but she wasn't going to.

Tall green hedges formed a labyrinth that she and Argantael had played in years ago. Noreia's pulse raced as she pushed through the hedges and into the foyer from the garden, determined to confront her father. When her father spun around to face her, his eyes flared with impatience.

Noreia stood her ground. "Father!" The words spilled out of the princess's mouth. "*I* will defend the dragons if you attack them." The king's eyes became huge and fiery at her defiance. "When I was little and there was a storm, you told me dragons were gentle and harmless. Now I know it's true, what you said. I know the dragon you captured on the beach today!"

"That dragon of which you speak so fondly is a vicious

beast," said her father. "He's been thrown into the dungeon. That's what happens to creatures who attack Emerhill!"

"No!" Noreia exclaimed, her worst fears confirmed.

"Noreia, listen to your father. Try to understand," said Queen Ceana, joining them in the foyer as heralding trumpets sounded on the terrace. "My heavens, that's for the guests, Roparz! They're early," cried the queen.

"Was it the seventh day after the first robin, or the eleventh day before the Spring Equinox occurs?" asked the king.

"Never mind, Roparz! We've invited them to stay here for Noreia's birthday, remember?"

Queen Ceana hurried out to the terrace to observe their guests arriving from Lismoire. Fairy guests were arriving in silver chariots, each pulled by a magnificent flock of doves. The wind blew the gossamer fabric of their capes, illuminated by the late afternoon sun. Each of the seven chariots landed upon the lawn near the terrace stairs.

Fairy kings and queens rode up in carriages pulled by regal unicorns, their bridles decorated with crystals that caught the light. Slowly, the unicorns arrived at the old forest gate. No footmen were necessary, as the luggage bounced over the air and up the terrace steps.

The queen rushed inside to receive her guests, ushering them into the hall. Noreia recognized her best friend Lisette's travel chest, as it floated through the hall and over to the stairs behind them. A thin elfin nobleman, wearing embroidered robes of silver damask silk, followed.

"Noreia! I've missed you. I'll be right down," called

Lisette from the stairs, "but I have so much to unpack."

Noreia called up to her friend, "Lisette! Now I have someone on my side. I need your help. Please, Lisette, tell them—"

"What's the matter?" asked Lisette, leaning over the banister.

"You are out of line, Noreia. The discussion is finished!" said King Roparz, pushing past his daughter.

"You must obey your father, the king. I would not test his patience again if I were you." Noreia's mother stood in front of her, so that the fairies couldn't hear them. Her expression became sober and concerned. "Noreia, you are not to say anything about this in front of our guests. Rudeness will not be tolerated here!"

Queen Ceana turned to the guests with a look of apology. "Please, come in. I apologize for the commotion."

"Greetings, Queen Perizada."

"Welcome, King Arne. Join me on the terrace, if you'd be so kind. It has a view of the sea, and today we may even see your island, Lismoire. We have much to plan." She threw a warning glance at her daughter and turned away.

Noreia and her father waited until the sounds of conversation diminished.

"You shouldn't have blamed Stalwart! It wasn't his fault!" Princess Noreia blurted out. She looked at the floor. "As for the dragons, you've made a mistake."

"Enough! My decision stands," said King Roparz, dismissing her with a hand wave. "Dragons are...*dragons!*"

"Please don't go. Father, please promise me you won't hurt them!"

"I am fed up with you, Noreia!" And with that, he grabbed her by the arm and pulled her to the foot of the stairs. "I'm taking you to your room."

"No!" Noreia shouted. "Let me stay! Why won't you listen to me? Let go!"

But her father dragged her up the stairs to her room, locking the door behind him. "You will stay here and do as your mother and I direct you, or you will have no home here at all!" King Roparz commanded his daughter.

Hearing the commotion, Lisette cried out, "Noreia!" and shed a single tear as she started down the stairs.

Noreia heard her father's shoes clumping down the stairs. It was unbearably silent outside her door, but soon she heard feet scuffling softly down the hallway. She recognized her brother's footsteps.

"P-s-s-s-t! Wait, Argantael!" There was more silence until she finally heard him reply.

"What?" he whispered. "What is going on? Why was everyone yelling?"

"Father locked me in my room. We had an argument."

"Why?"

"Because he doesn't want me to help the dragons. You'll help, won't you, Argantael?" Noreia pleaded. "That's it! *You've* got to find the key to the dungeon."

"The dungeon! Why me?"

"You are the only person who can," Noreia explained. "First, you'll need the plans for this castle. You'll find them in Father's map room. There's a cabinet on the left side of the wooden globe in the center of the room. Open the cabinet and pull out the first drawer. The scroll will be marked *Emerhill*."

"Okay. I'm going to casually stroll by the map room...."

"As casually as you can, and then just slip through the door."

"But what if someone sees me, Noreia?"

"Tell them you are looking for the aviary, Argantael," she said.

"Right. Aviary. I'm looking for the aviary. Can you direct me—" A guard's heavy footsteps resounded in the hallway.

"You'll have to hurry! Someone's coming. Go on!" Noreia urged.

Watching the door, the princess wondered how long she would have to wait. She thought of the number of plant varieties in the garden. Which plant had her grandmother used as a clue? She thought of annuals and perennials. She pondered shade dwellers versus flowers that needed full sun. What if her brother was questioned? Would her father ruin their plan? The party tomorrow! Noreia would have to have everything for her plan ready before then. Noreia was frantic by the time Argantael returned and slid some papers under the door.

She unfurled an architectural rendering and a plan view of Emerhill Castle, but the small drawing did not indicate any secret passageways to the dungeon. Her finger traced over the plan, the way she knew her father had done. When her finger moved over the doorway to Queen Gwenaelle's garden, she remembered the strange words her grandmother had spoken. "Leave no stone unturned." What did she mean? Her grandmother's garden had hundreds of cobblestones and pebbles. The rendering gave no indication of the placement of the topiaries or flowerbeds. Then she read the words "moon gate."

"Argantael, what do you know about archways? How do you make them curve like a full moon?" asked Noreia.

"Easy. There's this stone at the top called a keystone, and that holds the wedge shaped pieces together."

"That's it! I was trying to solve the mystery of the key to the dungeon. It's something about the keystone and the moon gate!" Noreia's eyes shone. "I think that is where Grandmother hid the key! It's under the keystone in the moon gate of the garden! If I had it, I could rescue Stalwart!"

"But you're locked in your room!" Argantael said through the door.

"Yes. So *you're* going to help me rescue him from the dungeon!" There was excitement in his sister's voice.

"How in the world can I?"

"*You* need to take the key from that garden," Noreia said.

"When? What if I get caught?"

"Tonight! Don't worry, you'll tip-toe out when everyone is asleep," said Noreia, "And if you find the key, put this iron lookalike in its place. It's the key to the broom closet. I knew it might come in handy someday." She passed the key under the door.

"Great idea!" said her brother." I'll hide the broom key

in my pocket for now. But where am I supposed to look for the key in the garden?"

"I'll draw a map for you." Noreia ran to find some parchment and a pen. After she made the sketch, she slid the parchment under the door.

"And the key is where?" asked Argantael.

"Where the X is on the map. Look for the midpoint of the arch in the moon gate, behind the fountain. It will be buried near that gate, under a plant."

"And all this time, you'll be locked up in your room?" her brother asked.

"I know you can do it. Whatever plant is beside the tiles under the archway is where you will dig. Find the plant, and dig up the key. Return the key to me tonight."

"My belly is in knots, Noreia. Are you sure no one will notice—"

"Remember, follow the path through the colonnade. It's risky being under the queen's balcony. Be sure to tiptoe."

That night, Noreia lay awake for hours, staring at the moonlight coming under the door and into her room. Finally, she heard Argantael step softly past her door and shuffle down the tower stairs.

She spent the next hour scared that her brother would be found out. If he were forced to give back the key, her plan to help Stalwart escape would be ruined! It seemed hours before she heard the scuffling of her brother's shoes again.

She stumbled to her feet and hurried to the bedroom door. There it was! An envelope with a key in it! She scrawled the word "*Thanks!*" on the envelope and pushed it back under the door. It was up to her now. She would have to be let out for her birthday. Tomorrow!

CHAPTER 7

The Fitting

Nissa swept open the heavy drapes to let in the waking sun. It was the second of May, Noreia's thirteenth birthday.

"Don't look now, Your Highness. We have company," said Nissa, glancing at the two guards at either side of the bedroom door. "Her Royal Majesty said it was for the best that you be escorted to breakfast." Nissa made a polite little curtsy.

Noreia felt a quiet sense of hope. This was the day she would rescue Stalwart and save the dragons. She leaped out of bed, put on her clothes, and went straight to where the royal family was gathered in the dining room. No sounds were uttered other than the occasional movement of a crepe fork.

"Sardines, Your Highness?" asked a royal butler with a tray.

Noreia kept thinking about the timing for her plan to free Stalwart. "Um, no, thank you." She would need Argantael's help to find the reference books for the journey. If she figured out a way to sneak out through the garden that evening.... What about the guards, though—?

Noreia saw her mother frown. "Princess Noreia, stop fidgeting! Sit up straight, *s'il vous plait.*"

"I'm sorry, Mother."

"Dear Noreia, pay attention. Why are your clothes so rumpled?" said Queen Ceana, taking a dainty bite of her crepe.

"Your mother is asking you a question, Noreia," said her father. "Did you fall asleep with your clothing on?" Noreia nodded, focusing on her plate.

"Can we talk about your journey to Dragonera, Roparz?" asked Queen Ceana. "Noreia will stay beside me, of course. She may keep me company while I finish my embroidery. I'm making a fine scarf for her to wear for the fall tournament." Noreia looked up from her plate. Her mother was adding berry preserves to a piece of toast. "Certain duties are appropriate for royal princes, whereas some are completely unsuitable for a princess. Must you take Argantael as well as Dalwyn?"

"Prince Argantael loves the spirit of adventure we share," the king chuckled. "That is why I plan to take him along, Ceana."

"Roparz! I agreed that *Dalwyn* may accompany you to Dragonera. Argantael is too young!" Queen Ceana didn't glance up from her plate.

"Ceana, I do not like these moods of yours!" said the king.

"Good day, then," said the queen. "And good day to those awful dragon creatures."

"Now, Ceana!"

"Now what! You want me to let you take my children away over dangerous waves? And for what? An adventure?"

The queen folded her napkin neatly, leaving behind the empty chair.

"Noreia, have you finished what is on your plate?" asked King Roparz.

"Yes, Father."

"The guards will escort you to your room. There, Nissa will prepare you for the birthday party your mother has planned. It's time you began behaving like a princess."

Once the guards had left her, Princess Noreia sat on the side of her bed and pondered. How could she think with these annoying guards following her everywhere? She only had control over her time at the party. And there was no time like the present. Noreia rushed to her bedside table. She yanked open a drawer, clutching the dungeon key and pressing it hard into her hand. What should she bring along? Preparing for a party is easy; just dress and you're ready. A voyage to a strange island with a dragon, however great, would require necessities.

Noreia stared at the armoire. If she went up to her room after the party, someone might notice her carrying a bag of clothing down.

She found a small tapestry purse her mother had given her. Then she rolled up a chemise, an old skirt, and a laced kirtle and threw them into the purse. She pulled out a roll of twine and an ancient arrowhead for fishing that her father had given her. What else? When the village church clock chimed three, she knew there was little time left to prepare for the party.

The tall mirror in her room threw back her frantic

expression and bedraggled hair. She would pretend nothing was out of the ordinary. She picked up her hairbrush and struggled with the tangles in her dark hair. She pulled again, and the worst knot was undone. She tossed the brush onto the bed, where it landed with a quiet thud.

Today was her birthday, but all she could think of was Stalwart. There was a knock at the door. Noreia answered and curtsied clumsily.

"*Gracious!* You're not dressed yet!" said her mother. Noreia's chambermaid, Nissa, stood next to the queen, holding a towel and a small bucket of well water.

The two entered and hurried to the ceramic washbasin.

Nissa poured some water into the basin. Noreia gave her hairbrush and comb to Nissa, who combed and arranged her hair. "We've already decided on your dress," said her mother, sitting on a bench at the foot of the bed. Nissa pulled a dress from the armoire. "No, not that one."

The queen held up a hand, walking around the dress that Nissa was holding like an appraiser, and put it back in the cupboard.

"Nissa, will you excuse us a moment, please?" The queen addressed the chambermaid but kept her eyes on her daughter. Nissa left the open armoire promptly, placing the hairbrush and comb on a table. "I think we can make a gown you'll like," said Queen Ceana, watching the chambermaid cross the room and close the door.

"Mother, Nissa was only trying to help," said Noreia. "Let me explain something to you, Noreia. You are a privileged girl in privileged circumstances. However, if I hear you mention that hunting voyage of your father's to any of our guests, you will remain in this room for the duration of your own party," said the queen.

"Mother, I never—"

"Even Lisette and her family must never know!" said her mother. "If the fairies learn of Emerhill's plan to defeat the dragons, we could have an international incident. On my watch, we won't have any."

"But Lisette and I...." said Noreia, taking a breath.

"Do you understand?" Noreia's mother was stern and direct. "Otherwise, I'll cancel the whole party if I must!" There was a terrible pause. "Is that clear?"

"Yes, Mother."

"Let's get you dressed properly, at least."

As Queen Ceana snapped her fingers, a row of seamstresses filed into the room. The first held a tape measure, a basket of notions, and a pincushion tied onto her wrist. The second carried several bolts of bright fabric. The third carried a portable wooden writing desk, a jar of ink, and a quill. Following them, a merchant carried a neat stack of large red velvet boxes containing sparkling strands of jewelry.

"Does Mademoiselle prefer silk, satin, or velvet?" began the seamstress with the writing desk, the quill in her hand.

"Um, silk is very nice, I think," said the princess.

"Write down that the princess will have nothing but the finest French velvet and Chinese brocades!" said the queen.

"Thank you, Mother. That sounds lovely!" said Noreia.

"Do you want blue, pink, olive, teal, violet, crimson,

turquoise, or goldenrod fabric?" asked the seamstress.

"Any color that you have, if it's not too much trouble," the princess said.

"The princess will need a teal green velvet underdress, edged with the finest golden velvet cording. The overdress will be of gold silk brocade, and she will need to choose a pair of embroidered shoes."

Within minutes, a bolt of fabric was over her head and nimble seamstresses pinned and draped the fabric. Half the group sat in a circle and stitched away with lightning speed, while the jewelry merchant chose a pair of emerald earrings to match Noreia's eyes.

"We'll need someone who is good with hair. Louis? Pierre?" asked the queen.

"Your Highness would be most pleased with Monsieur Claude. His work can transform a haystack into a strand of pearls!" said the head seamstress.

In a moment, Monsieur Claude himself strolled in. "I think...a little lift here at the sides, a generous sweep to the left and a few curls here for balance—" Monsieur Claude found himself interrupted.

"I think something classic will be much preferred in this case," said the queen. Monsieur Claude was hesitant to smile, but he managed a nod of his head before standing back to reconsider his task. Resuming his work, he swept Noreia's dark hair back with one hand while giving it a gentle brush with the other. He braided a strand interspersed with freshwater pearls on each side of her head. He pulled the hair into a loose twist, holding it back with a golden comb. Then he added a cap of golden cording and pearls.

"Will you be needing anything else, Your Highness?" Nissa asked.

The princess found herself in front of her mirror. She was surprised by the effect.

"Mother, what do you think? Mother?" Noreia hadn't noticed her mother leave the room. She stared at the strange new reflection in the mirror. Her silky hair was held back into a lovely twist that fell upon her shoulders. Her underdress was a long sleeved gown of green velvet. Her gold brocade overdress was laced up the back. Noreia admired its formfitting, laced sleeves. Her gold bejeweled belt matched the golden slippers on her feet. She looked beautiful in the current French style, but in no way prepared for a dragon rescue.

"Thank you so much, Nissa," said Noreia. "That will be all."

Only once Nissa and the seamstresses had left the room did Noreia pull open the drawer to her night table and place the dungeon key in her drawstring purse.

CHAPTER 8

A Banquet of Languages

A second later, there was another knock at the door.

Noreia jumped. She took in a breath and opened the door carefully. The queen was waiting. "I'm glad you decided to join us," she said warmly.

"It's still early, Mother," Noreia said.

"It's four o'clock. We'll begin the evening early, to make

time for your father's announcement," said the queen. "Noreia, I have a special gift for you. It belonged to your father's mother, Grandmother Marcelina." She stood behind her daughter to join the clasp of a delicate gold locket.

"Will Grandmother Marcelina be at the party?"

"No, she is busy with her work. She lives alone beside the sea." The princess's mother held her close, but Noreia pulled away.

"By the sea?" Noreia didn't realize she was speaking aloud.

"Noreia, what's the matter?" her mother asked.

"Why doesn't she visit me on my birthday?" Noreia inquired.

"Your father's mother has a special quality you will learn about one day. You are growing so fast! Be careful, Noreia, or you'll forget to enjoy the time you have now. Thirteen doesn't last, dear," said her mother. Her mother's smiling eyes met hers. Queen Ceana was wearing Turkish robes edged with gold cords. She wore her hair up, arranged with pheasant feathers and jeweled salamanders. "Noreia, remember, I'm counting on you to behave."

"Yes, Mother. I'll do my best," said Noreia.

Her mother motioned to the three guards at the top of the stairs. She directed one to stay on the landing and the two others to walk with them. Noreia pretended to admire her hair and new necklace in the upstairs hall mirror as she listened to her mother talking to them.

"You two must make sure that my daughter does nothing

foolish today. Every private discussion of hers is of importance to me." Noreia made sure her drawstring purse was held tight in her hand.

As the two guards led them to the Great Hall, Noreia reached up to touch her necklace. Her mother walked at her side. She loved her mother, and was grateful for the gift. Would she really have to leave her?

"Thank you," said Noreia, glancing back. As Noreia and the queen entered the hall from the alabaster stairs, her mother's countenance changed. Her chin rose, and her shoulders went back. Her smile turned to a serious expression.

A peal of applause and comments of *"Bellissimo!"* *"Très chic!"* and *"Muy elegante!"* filled the hall. But Noreia was disheartened. It was unthinkable to be in such surroundings when Stalwart needed her.

A hundred guests strolled through the hall on the inlaid-marble floor, flanked by seven foot high silver candelabras. Exotic songbirds hopped between branches, hung artfully along the southeast wall. More songbirds perched upon the centerpiece of the banquet table. Elfin noblemen from India and their wives arrived, butterflies of Africa hovering around their shoulders. Turbaned ladies from African lands strolled arm in arm with dukes and marquises from Burgundy and Toulouse.

An African chief and his fairy daughter approached. She wore a patterned mud cloth gown and a coral necklace. Her hair was woven into elegant braids set with tiny orange tourmaline crystals. Her wings were luminescent and sparkling.

"Queen Ceana, how many years have passed? May I present my daughter, Adisa? I'm sorry my wife, Kamaria, could not attend. She is receiving guests tonight on Fay Linn Island and sends her regrets."

"Thank you, Chief Emem. Yes, it has been a great many years since the Alliance of the Fairy Realms. Your daughter is lovely," Queen Ceana said with a royal nod.

"I'm pleased to make your acquaintance," said Noreia, who had followed her mother through the crowd. She nodded as well, as Princess Adisa curtsied.

"Let me introduce you to some of my favorite dishes, Princess Adisa," said the queen. The queen escorted her over to the table to find her placecard.

Gentlemen in hose and satin doublets bowed to ladies of China cooling themselves with delicate fans.

"Princess Ying, may I present my daughter, Princess Noreia," said the queen, approaching a young lady wearing a long embroidered silk dress and jacket. Her smooth black hair was held in a sculptural knot. While admiring the tall candelabras and royal tapestries with awe, Princess Ying smiled at Noreia.

"*Enchanted*," said Noreia. She tried to appear alert, with nothing on her mind but the joy of seeing family and friends at the celebration.

"Would you like to take a walk in the gardens, Princess Ying?" asked the queen. "The irises are blooming." Noreia's thoughts could not help drifting to Stalwart in the dungeon. *What would become of him?* Her mother nudged her, bringing her back to the present.

"Uh, sorry," said Noreia. "I'll take you for a stroll if you'd like." Noreia took Princess Ying's hand, and they strolled toward the doors to the garden. The French doors revealed peacocks, swans, and egrets bathing in the pond and preening their feathers.

"Princess Ying, I am so honored to meet you. My grandmother planted most of this walled garden herself. Here are the irises."

"Lovely. Did you know the iris is a Chinese native flower?" said Princess Ying.

"It's beautiful," said Princess Noreia.

"Here," said Princess Ying, "is a gateway that reminds me of my home." She admired the gate, the round hand-laid circle of flagstones.

"Your grandmother honors my country! The round gate is called a moon gate. Our palace in China has similar entranceways. Each of the stones was handmade and placed without mortar."

There was that phrase again, *moon gate*—a beautiful gate that brought to Noreia's mind, of course, an image of Stalwart, the majestic dragon in the dungeon. Below the gate's keystone was where her brother had unearthed the key, and the key would set Stalwart free.

The blare of trumpets pulled her from her thoughts. "Shall we return to the banquet?" Noreia asked her new friend.

"Of course," said Princess Ying.

The two girls walked back to the terrace. There wasn't time to reach the dungeon now. Noreia would have to wait until the guests were distracted. Then she could ask Argantael for help. She needed him to get her into the library quickly, because half an hour had already gone by.

The guests of honor arrived. Queen Perizada appeared in a grand archway. Her crown of white coral was decorated with Oriental pearls and shells from the Indian Ocean. As she descended the stairs, seven elves with conch shell trumpets announced her arrival. She took the hand of King Arne, the Fairy King of the Realm of the Sky, who led her along the steppingstones as if she were floating.

Two more princesses followed them. First came Lisette, in a medieval golden satin gown. Then came her sister, Fayette, with a basket of flower petals. She scattered the petals upon the terrace, and passed by the royal guests.

When Fairy King Arne and Fairy Queen Perizada took the floor, the crowd stared in wonder as Queen Perizada's bright yellow wings fanned for a moment. She blew in Queen Ceana's direction a strange apparition that became a spray of exotic flowers. A tabor began a slow dance, called a pavane, for them. Queen Perizada and her elfin husband glided over the floor like a boat upon the calmest sea. The guests stood in quiet fascination.

Noreia knew she wouldn't find a better time to disappear, find Argantael, and prepare to fly to Dragonera with Stalwart. She slipped through the crowd, past an antechamber leading to the garden courtyard, and into the dining room, where Argantael was talking with Princess Adisa.

"Princess Adisa, I see you have met my younger brother, Prince Argantael."

"I'm enchanted to meet him," said the princess. "Look. Lady Flora is talking to Lady Yvette. She's wearing a tall hat, called a henin, in the butterfly style. I've never seen one before!"

A gong resounded. Two Chinese military warriors put up their swords and escorted Mystic Queen Jia stepped into the room, escorted by her husband, Emperor Jun, both wearing layers of bright yellow and red Chinese satin robes.

"*Excusez-moi*, Your Imperial Majesties, Aunt Jia and Uncle Jun. I am honored to welcome you," said Noreia.

"We are delighted, Noreia," said her great Aunt Jia.

"Argantael, there's someone I want you to meet."

"What? I was speaking with Princess Adisa," said Argantael.

"Argantael, I must speak with you, now," Noreia insisted.

"Not now, Noreia. They are about to release the butterflies!"

Noreia slipped her hand into Argantael's and pulled him into an antechamber.

CHAPTER 9

Treasuring Knowledge

The sun was getting lower on the horizon, its golden rays sparkling in the goblets and platters.

"What in the world do you want?" Argantael asked.

"I need to get into Father's library," Noreia said urgently.

"You are truly loony, Noreia!"

"Father has books on every subject of importance. He must have a handbook or manual about how to survive on a tropical island. I have to get in there."

"No. Father's library? If he finds out, he'll force me to recite my French verbs backwards. He'll never let me borrow his atlases again, and I can say goodbye to conversational Greek lessons."

"You are the only one who is familiar enough with the king's library. You can find what I need for the journey. Please help me, Argantael."

"You'll owe me a favor," Argantael said. "A big favor, like helping me to stay out of trouble this time."

"Thank you. You are the best brother in the world!" She hugged him.

"What exactly am I doing?" he asked her, his voice sounding more alert.

"Follow me," she said. She grabbed his hand again. They walked from the castle corridors into the garden courtyard under balconies draped with wisteria. Along the enclosed walkway, they crept by the life sized stone statues of important fairy folk.

"Noreia, I think we really shouldn't—"

And then they both heard him. A guard was patrolling the corridor. With the heavy armor he was wearing, they could hear each footstep coming closer. Argantael pulled his sister by the sleeve through an archway. They hid behind a topiary tree.

Rattle-thump! Rattle-thump! Another guard arrived from the opposite direction. The two guards passed each other, pivoted, and stopped.

"Did you find the intruder?" asked the tall guard with a deep voice. It echoed in the corridor.

"I'll check the throne room," said the other guard, "while you check the locks."

Rattle-thump, stomp! Rattle-thump! Thump! Thump!

"Do you know where Father hides the key?" Noreia whispered, shaking.

"Easy."

"How is that?"

"I have a copy." Argantael pulled a key from the pocket of his tunic. He used his key in the heavy oak paneled door to the library. The door creaked open, and the two siblings stepped into their father's lair.

Worn and dusty leather books filled the shelves. A stone fireplace dominated the room, along with a weaponry case with archery bows and Celtic swords. The study had a strong scent of fresh tobacco that permeated the Persian rugs and velvet cushions. Aside from the light from the outdoors, the room was in shadow.

Their father's collections were everywhere. The swords' sheaths sparkled with silver Celtic knots and dragons with ruby eyes. The books on the shelves were interspersed with dragon teeth, crystal rocks, and a dusty globe on a rotating wooden stand. There were engravings on the walls of flora and fauna with Latin names. A Chinese abacus and a Spanish glazed majolica plate were displayed upon another wall. A paneled folding screen stood by the grand vaulted windowsill. It was draped with the leather strap of a jeweled scabbard with a gilded sword. Above them, was a coved wooden ceiling of square panels. Sculpted marble egrets holding branches of dragon's-claw willow decorated the archway above the door.

Argantael approached a shelf of books. As he pulled a volume from the shelf, it released a cloud of dust. "Grandmother told me once that this room was built by our great grandfather, who was the finest architect of his clan."

"Rattle-thump! Rattle-step, rattle-step, rattle-step! Swoosh-thump!"

Argantael put his hand over his sister's mouth. Slowly, they made their way behind the screen and backed up against the wall, trying to be invisible. They heard an un-pleasant sound, more unsettling than the first: the clanging of a metal key ring and the clinking of a key in the lock.

"Here, let me try!" said the deep voice. The clattering in the key plate kept them alert and silent.

"Never mind that, we have to report what we heard," said the other guard.

"Let's forget about it," the deep voice responded.

"I suppose you're right. We were just hearing things." The royal siblings' mouths dropped, as rattling signaled the guards' departure. Argantael resumed the conversation in a whisper.

"You'll need a book on survival skills. Food, where would you find...hmmm, gardening, gathering and gold mining, growing...." Argantael ran an index finger over the gold leaf books. "How about something by Annwyn Primula? She writes the Castle and Garden series called *Cottages in Collaboration*." He stood on the ladder, calling down to her. Argantael pulled some books from the shelf and tossed them onto the carpet with a thud.

"Too advanced, I think."

"Here, Noreia, try *Building a Makeshift Dwelling*, by Garrett Green."

"Where did you find that one?" Noreia smiled.

"I looked under 'Building.' It was right next to *A Shipwreck Manual*."

"Perfect! But I have to choose, because I can only fit one into my bag," Noreia said.

"Footsteps!" they both whispered at once. They froze. It was only the sound of an upstairs door creaking.

"Whew! Hand me the one about green dwellings, and let's get out of here," Noreia whispered. She put it in her purse. Then she picked up the stray books and handed them up to her brother, who replaced them quickly by the authors' last names.

A fanfare of trumpets nearly knocked Argantael off the ladder. The siblings' wide eyes met.

"The king's announcement!" They slipped out into the cool breezeway, before the guards' footsteps were too close, locked the library door, and hurried to the throne room.

There, the siblings split up and tried to blend into the crowd of partygoers.

"Your attention, please!" shouted a brocaded royal courtier, who waited for the chatter in the room to diminish. "The king wishes to make a statement!" King Roparz rose from his chair, lifting a pewter mug. Applause filled the room as the king gently tapped his goblet with a spoon. "My friends from many lands! I thank you all for attending my daughter's thirteenth birthday party. A toast to you, my loving daughter!" Minstrels played an introduction as people craned their heads to locate her.

"Where is she?" asked the queen.

"Here I am," called Noreia. She faked a smile.

The applause subsided. "It is also my great pleasure," the king continued, "to announce our plan to set sail tomorrow for the undiscovered territory of Dragonera Island! My eldest son, Dalwyn, will accompany me. There, we will begin a scientific expedition to explore the, um, land of the dragons!" As the king took his seat, a silence stayed in the room.

What could she do? Noreia couldn't allow her father to attack the dragons on their own island. She followed her parents to the buffet, where they started talking in low voices behind a marble column.

"Everyone is sitting down, Roparz. There'll be an empty seat if your mother doesn't show up," said the queen.

"Marcelina lives life her own way, alone in a sea cottage, by herself! But I wish she would take the time to be here for her granddaughter," said the king.

"Would Your Majesty like an appetizer?" asked a waiter with a tray full of delicacies.

"No, thank you," said the king. As a wave of ladies swept in their direction like an unwelcome rain cloud, Noreia heard the treble of their chattering. It sounded like a series of wind instruments played out of key.

"Every year, a royal international competition decides on the most beautiful hat. I was admiring the ladies' steeple hats," Lady Alaia was saying. Indeed, the women surrounding them wore high conical hats with gauzy, sweeping veils.

"Did you see Lady Fleurette's high hat? What a charming veil!" said a second lady.

"Well, I certainly have a chance. Mine is based upon the arc of a vaulted ceiling," said Lady Yvette.

"Mine is based upon the curve of the River Seine in Paris," said another lady. They chattered on.

Noreia's eyes wandered as the dignitaries and nobles found their seats at the banquet table, a long oak table draped in the finest tasseled silks. A hundred settings with carved quartz goblets and golden utensils awaited the world dignitaries. In the center of the table was a great climbing wisteria vine, wound around a Corinthian column. The vine had curled its way up to and around the wooden eaves above them, its white blooms scenting the air. Hummingbirds flitted around the vines. Minstrels played their reed flutes merrily as a troupe of Chinese acrobats performed.

Noreia slipped out to the lush garden, alive with the sound of crickets. She glanced back at her friends from beyond the terrace, clapping as the butterflies were released. She had only dreamed of such a party. It wasn't difficult to leave the crowd, because she couldn't stand their banter, so easily uttered as Stalwart suffered. How easy it was to ignore a fellow creature! How easy it would be to slip back into her princess world again. Yet there he was, her friend Stalwart, alone and hurt in the dungeon. On she would run, straight to Stalwart, to release him from his prison!

CHAPTER 10

The Dungeon Beckons

Noreia slipped past a guard enraptured with the music. He was looking up as strokes of orange light painted the sky. She dashed through the open terrace door and hurtled down the stairs two at a time. She could hear a voice singing a ballad, accompanied by a gittern and a reed pipe.

Noreia sped on. She reached the privacy of her grandmother's garden. The key clanged against the gate. Open! In the far corner, she pulled away a layer of ivy to uncover an imposing iron gate. She put the iron key in the lock and turned it. Tugging the squeaking gate open with one hand, she slipped through the gateway.

"Hello!" Only her echo responded. The iron door squeaked and clanged with a rever berating slam.

She followed the ivy covered walls to the dungeon. It was near the foot of a flight of stairs. The place smelled musty and damp.

"Stalwart?"

She crept through a hallway of iron bars. The sunlight followed her, peeking over her shoulders. As she peered into each vacant cell, Noreia called through the coolness of the air.

"Stalwart!"

The setting sun cascaded over the stony walls and across the chiseled stone pavers of the floor. The groaning of a wounded creature echoed.

"Is anyone here?" Noreia called out. Suddenly, she was plunged into darkness, as the sun dropped below her, the castle walls, and the golden sea.

"Princess, you've found me!" At the sound of Stalwart's voice, Noreia gasped. She looked down upon the cobblestone floor and felt the icy chill. An early moon washed its light upon the floor through a small window near the ceiling, casting shadows of the iron bars on the dungeon walls.

"Young princess, where are you?" His deep and tired voice rumbled inside the prison walls.

Noreia hurried to reach the end of the empty prison row. Stalwart lay in shadow on the stone floor, a glaze of white light moving over the scales on his tail. In the path of the moon, his huge body seemed smaller, huddled in the corner of an enormous cell.

"Stalwart! I'd know your voice anywhere!"

"I am grateful for your kindness, Princess," said the great dragon." I knew you would return to me."

"You are my friend, Stalwart." She entered the cell and found the arrow wound on Stalwart's torso. The bleeding had stopped. On his long neck, his head turned slowly so that he could look into her eyes. "We still have time to evade the guards, Stalwart. Soon you'll be on your island again, and I will stay with you!"

The princess saw how frail the dragon was. The sheen of his scales was dull. His teal eyes no longer glowed with radiant light. His wings no longer captured the moon light. His huge body showed the curve of his ribs.

"The wound is healing, but I am a prisoner here. In your kingdom, I will always be feared." Noreia's tears fell upon his neck. The great dragon closed his eyes and sighed.

"I've got to get you out of here, Stalwart!" she whispered. The dragon looked back at her with the saddened eyes of defeat. "Stalwart, let's go. I've come to free you!"

"I can no longer go with you, Princess. I'm too weak, and I must rest now.

"Stalwart, we can't let them win this time! You and I will fly away with the wind at our backs. We can start a new life together. No one can stop us when they see your broad wings in flight!"

The room seemed to hold more shadows than before. Noreia felt a strange fog moving in. The moist fog slipped through the iron bars, and the cobblestone floor was painted silver by the full moon. The fog glowed from within, the way a full moon projects its cool blue light through clouds.

When there was no response, she knew. Her hands clasped over her mouth, and she sank into despair. She slumped to the cold floor. She lay there, unmoving, until her sobs subsided. He was gone.

Noreia's tears spilled out like rivers. She felt her heart turning cold, a heart that had believed in her father's love.

In that moment, she gave up her tenderness for him. She would be a warrior her father feared, as she had feared him.

The moon shone against the calming sky. It gleamed like a white orb through the window near the ceiling. The night was clear.

Noreia stopped her racing thoughts. Her tears ceased. She dried them on her long sleeve and left the dungeon as she had entered it, unseen. She locked the door behind her and climbed up the back stairway to the terrace.

Her plan was ruined. She saw the cruelty of her father's eyes in her mind. There was no way out this time, except on her father's ship. Her parents would never allow her to go on the expedition, but if she hid on the ship while the crew was asleep, she might have a chance. Losing the dragon she loved built a growing sense of defiance in Noreia. She could save dragonkind.

"Noreia, I've been looking everywhere for you!" said Lisette, startling Noreia.

"How did you know where to find me, Lisette?" asked Noreia in a fearful tone.

"I used the wayfaring spell. I can use it only three times in my life as a fairy. It allows me to traverse by way of the spirit world to wherever my friends are in trouble!" Lisette explained.

"I can't stay here. I must go," said Noreia, embracing her friend tightly.

"Are you leaving? Where? I don't understand you. Tell them you're sorry, Noreia, for that senseless argument with your father, and that you didn't mean it. Your father wants the best for you, the kingdom—"

"He doesn't! He wants to kill all the magical dragons, Lisette. And they are your protectors, the ancient guards of your Fairy Realm."

"Noreia, I don't believe you. You're angry, you—" Lisette looked up as gray clouds covered the moon.

"It's the truth. He's thrown Stalwart, my dragon friend, into the dungeon. He was trying to fish in our bay when an Emerhill ship fired at him. And now he is dead! He will have died for nothing if I don't go to help them." The sky was streaked with lavender clouds, as long shadows loomed over the stone statues on the terrace.

"Then let me go with you. They are my fairy ancestors' protectors, not yours."

"I don't think you'd survive the journey, Lisette. You are not as strong as I am."

"I must help you, Noreia." Worry and concern was apparent on Lisette's face. Noreia quickened her pace across the lawn, toward the trees. "I need to fight when no one else can!" she said.   Lisette hastened after Noreia to the end of the great lawn, only to stop, outrun.

From the lawn, the great harbor stretched out before the sea as boats moved upon the water. "Wait! Your place is with your parents, and mine."

"Don't follow me, I can look after myself!"

"Noreia, don't take the path to the beach, because your father's ship is there in the harbor. He has stationed guards at every—"

"Father's hunting grounds! I'll go through the forest, then," Noreia said.

"At least take my cloak!" Lisette said, catching up with her friend. Princess Noreia threw Lisette's wool cloak around her own shoulders and hugged her.

"I'm sorry, Lisette. I'll return, my friend," she said. "It's something I need to do. I must save the dragons!"

"I know, Noreia, but if you are lost in the dark forest, will you send for help?" Lisette called as her friend ran to the mossy steps where King Roparz' hunting grounds began.

Noreia hastened toward a crumbling ivy covered archway. Beyond a flight of stairs and another archway was the beckoning forest.

CHAPTER 11
The Wild Forest

Moonbeams blinked through the trees as the forest trail turned. Owls in high branches scattered through the trees as Noreia ran, treading over snapping twigs toward the deepest part of the woods. She held Lisette's cloak around her shoulders as the wind picked up.

Low branches swayed in the wind as she reached a clearing. The cold wind enveloped her shoulders. Noreia caught her breath. The coolness of the forest surrounded her. She stood in amazement, for she had not taken these few steps before. Merely ten minutes from the castle, she felt miles away from her father's commands. Had she gone too far? Great oaks towered over the princess, ancient and protective. Deep shadows and moonlight dappled the ground.

The clearing looked out over grassy squares of farmland. A winding path led to Emerhill village, where half timbered houses made of mud, straw, plaster, and timber spotted the land.

Hearing the sound of the horn to summon the royal guards, she seized her chance. Princess Noreia knew she had to run. She dropped a hair ribbon near a fork in the trail to baffle the guards. Another path led through the trees, where she could easily lose them. She had to reach the first royal ship before its voyage to Dragonera. It would leave for the island at dawn. If the guards caught her, she wouldn't be able to stow away. Someone had to defend the dragons.

She heard the frenetic sound of branches and brush as the soldiers thrashed their way through to locate the path she had taken. Noreia ran off the trail, ducking under branches.

A footpath wound along the hillside, down to a creek. Huge boulders covered in moss led her over the trickling stream. Thorny blackberries blocked her path, their branches hanging and twisting over the water.

A stag with majestic antlers gazed at her from the embankment. A halo of moonlight shone through the birches behind him. He held her gaze when she looked at him, as if telling her he would protect and defend her. She would be careful with the trust of the animals and fairies. He turned, and his fawns trotted behind. The evening wind blew leaves through the air, and the moon shone in an arc behind a grassy hill.

She heard deep voices as the guards whacked away at the vines in their way. Afraid the guards were coming too close, Noreia glanced back.

"Your Highness, wait! You must stop, please," she heard a guard say as he groped through the stray branches.

She sprinted forward, through branches and trailing foliage thicker still, as her mother's voice leapt to mind.

"You must obey your father, the king." Then her father's voice reverberated in her brain. "Leading only the finest, you must battle and destroy every last dragon!" As she recalled the statements she had heard, her emotions surfaced. She threw the branches and foliage from her path with a determination fueled by anger.

When she peered back through the thick branches, the bright gold of the guards' uniforms caught her eye. Just then she toppled and fell into the creek. She shivered, muddy and dripping, stumbling to her feet.

As her eyes adjusted to the darkness, Noreia found that she was lost in the forest. Running along the embankment, she scanned the hillside. The quiet village of Emerhill nestled somewhere in the soft distant hills. She might find it where the creek ran into the sea. She crossed a patch of weeds and found the water as it trickled toward the mossy shore. Looking back again, she saw the guards' torches blinking away in a snaking motion through the distant trees. She had escaped them!

Leaves strewn upon the ground disguised her current trail. Amber light shone through the canopy of leaves as she ran back and forth through the birches. She wiped her watery eyes with her sleeve and gasped for air. She was compelled to go on, but her exhaustion held her. She collapsed upon a low rock beside the creek, splashing her face with the cool water.

She lifted her hand from the dank tree roots below the surface of the creek. The sound of frogs and crickets surrounded her. She was alone.

"Dear me!" said a voice. Noreia jumped up and turned to see a woman carrying a firewood bundle upon her back. "I may need to sit here awhile," she said.

"Doesn't your family help you gather wood?" Noreia asked her.

"No. I'm certain of that. I'm widowed, you see. No children in the house, dear," said the woman.

"I'm sorry."

"Don't be. My husband died fifteen years ago. The walking is good for my strength."

"Where do you live?" asked Noreia. "It's well past sunset now."

"I live in a small place near the water's shore."

"You climbed so far to get here. Why?"

"Not far for me. I'm as strong as an ox."

"May I help you?" asked Noreia. "That wood looks very heavy."

"Thank you!" said the woman. "I just need help to carry this wood as far as the edge of the forest. I can make the rest of the way myself."

"Then we can help each other. I'm lost here, and you will be guiding me," said Noreia. She placed the bundle behind her shoulders and tied it around her ribs. The moon provided a small amount of light between the trees. Noreia followed the woman down a path. The village was in the near distance. A few half-timbered dwellings were perched along the cliff. Men carried bundles of branches or drove carts over the seaside path to their homes.

The luminous moon was peeking over the sand when the

two reached the rocky beach. The woman pointed to a stone cottage with a thatched roof standing by the shore. As Noreia looked where the woman was pointing, she was aware of a strange and wonderful transformation. The woman's ragged clothes fell away to reveal a radiant fairy. She arose like a flower from the earth, while seawater twinkled like sparkling crystals from her dress of lichen threaded with cobwebs.

Her sparkling cloak spread over the ground like a web of fallen leaves. She carried a wand of birch, silver, and crystal. Her soft gray wings fluttered like a cabbage butterfly's.

"Where do you want to go?"

The fairy's brown eyes sparkled as Noreia stepped back, awestruck and bewildered. The magical lady emanated a green white light, like the moon. Her rays fell upon every leaf, tree trunk, and flower about her. "Do not be afraid. I am Fairy Rayenna, Noreia."

Noreia thought she might be lost in a dream, or too exhausted to think. "Are you here to help me?"

"Yes, because you helped me."

"Why doesn't Father help the dragons?"

"He fears the dragons' power. They are strong in magic. Humans are afraid of them," said the fairy.

"I must reach my father's ship, which sets sail tomorrow for Dragonera."

"Follow this sloping trail along the beach. Ask the fishermen for Marcelina's cottage. I know she misses you."

The fairy put an opalescent green pearl in Noreia's hand.

"Hold onto this pearl! An ancient prophecy states that if the dragons' power is revived, order will be restored in the Sea Realm as well. Once the Four Fairy Realms are saved, the delicate magic of the fairies will unite all the Realms," Fairy Rayenna explained with a wave of her crystal wand.

"Wait a minute. How in the world do I bring the four Fairy Realms together?" asked the princess.

"If you ever need to call upon one of the fairy elders, you may roll this pearl on a flat surface. Remember and be warned! Do not use the green pearl's power unless all other plans have failed you!"

"I understand," said Noreia. The fairy vanished into a ray of light with a fluttering of her great transparent wings.

Noreia opened her hand and placed the green pearl securely in her pocket. She saw that the fairy had also left her a beautiful book covered in gilded leather, lying upon her cape. She turned the book over to read the title. *A Traveler's Companion to the Fairy Dominions*, Volume I, by Annwyn Primula. The second chapter described the isle of Dragonera.

"DRA-GON-ER-A: *An island uninhabited by man, where the creatures of the sea live and thrive. Historically, large scaled creatures of the air, called dragons, were sighted near the island.*"

For a moment, Noreia's mind fell into the pages, immersed in the history of magical folk. Diminutive fairies slept inside tulips, lilies, and hen's eggs. Fairies with fins lived in ponds under the water's surface. Moss dwellers burrowed themselves under the roots of oak trees. Then she remembered her task and looked at the cottage to which the fairy had pointed. A light in a window guided her to the front door. Noreia knocked. An elderly woman in a knitted shawl answered, holding a lantern high to look at the princess.

"What do you need, my dear?" she asked.

"I'm lost. I was hoping you could help me?" Noreia asked. The woman had a familiar face. Noreia's eyes lit up, recognizing the woman who had helped raise her. "Grandmother?"

"Well, now. I thought there might be something you need. I've been waiting for you, Noreia," said Marcelina.

"How did you know we would meet?" Noreia asked, bewildered. "I knew from the stars, my dear. The stars are always truthful."

CHAPTER 12

The Woman by the Sea

"Enter, out of the damp, dear," Grandmother Marcelina said. "We've had quite a cold spell lately, and a few light rains. It's too chilly now, even for early spring. Don't you agree?" Leading Noreia to a place by the fire, the woman covered her with a woolen blanket.

The quaint cottage was filled with decorations. Crocheted shawls and straw hats hung upon the wall pegs.

A few lit candles dripped wax into tiny holders. Pewter plates leaned against the fireplace mantle. A pair of the woman's clogs was placed upon the hearth.

"Were you expecting me?" asked Noreia, taking off her cloak.

"You won't find another house for miles along this coast. Yes, I hoped you'd come here one day," said the woman.

"I had long ago forgotten about this cottage. I've missed you so much, Grandmother!" Noreia said.

"Dear child." The old woman stroked Noreia's hair with her aged fingers. "It's so good to see you growing up to be a kind girl. Let yourself be comfortable. Take off your shoes and stay here by the fireplace." The woman had the kind smile Noreia remembered, and eyes with a sparkling gentleness.

"Can you help me?" asked Noreia. She slipped off her sopping evening slippers at the hearth and shivered.

The woman beamed a smile. "I have made my special soup for you. I'm delighted that a grandchild of my own has come to visit me."

"Grandmother, I cannot stay with you. I've got to get on the ship leaving at dawn!"

Noreia embraced her. Then, seated at a weathered table covered with a patterned tablecloth, she related the story of her quest to her grandmother. The woman served her a bowl of soup from an iron pot hanging over the kitchen fire. The dish had the aroma of shallots and fresh dill, lemon and garlic. Forgetting her worries, Noreia dipped in her spoon and swallowed the soup, made from mussels and clams. "This soup is warm and delicious!" said Noreia between mouthfuls of hot broth.

"Eat well, child," said her grandmother with a smile.

"There's so much I need to tell you, and so many questions to ask."

"I'm glad that our paths have crossed again, my child," said Grandmother Marcelina. "I used to live in Emerhill Castle when you were a baby. How I loved you."

"Why didn't you visit me in the castle, Grandmother?"

"Your grandfather liked to fish. He loved the ocean. He preferred to be in this little house with me. When he died, I stayed in this little cottage, where I could watch the sea," said her grandmother. "Sit here by the fire with me and I'll weave you a yarn or two."

"Please don't go to any trouble to make me something. I'm sure my clothes will be dry soon," said the young girl. "I have to leave for the ship before dawn."

Marcelina laughed and beamed. "*To weave a yarn* is an old expression, Noreia. It means to weave a story. Telling a story is like weaving something."

Marcelina's hands were still, and she sat back and gazed into the flickering fireplace.

"Tell me about my father, Grandmother. What was he like at my age?" asked Noreia.

"Well, what do you think? You are his daughter."

"I think he must have been stubborn and angry most of the time. Maybe he didn't like to be around people," said Noreia, folding her arms.

"You're wrong, Noreia. He loved the sea and its many

creatures, and he and I were close. He adored hearing stories about the early days. From time to time, he did forget about people. He liked to run through the forest. He used to get splinters from climbing trees."

"Why doesn't he like dragons, Grandmother?" asked Noreia.

"Every young boy loves dragons, but there comes a day when they all seem to find they fear them. What we love changes, Noreia. What matters is that *you* care about them, don't you?"

"Of course," said the girl.

The cottager's heavy eyes twinkled in the firelight as she looked up from her knitting.

"Grandmother, I'm not brave and wise, the way you are. I'm only a young girl!"

"Only a child! Now, let me tell you something. Your mother comes from a long line of fairy ancestors. And they are a part of you, Noreia."

"But my mother and father are mortals. They are rulers of Emerhill Kingdom, but they are not magical."

"Listen, child. Your mother and Queen Perizada are sisters. You and Princess Adisa are cousins, first cousins."

"First cousins, and—is my mother a *fairy?*"

"Yes, Noreia, yes. And you are her daughter. You must find the strength within to do what you must do. And you are not alone! Do you know about Xiang, the eldest dragon? His magic is as old as the sea is deep." Marcelina leaned over to her basket of yarn.

"Who?"

"Hasn't your father ever told you of Xiang?" Marcelina was winding the fine gray wool into a ball.

"Yes, he did," Noreia remembered, sitting back in her chair.

"Xiang is the dragon lord of fog." Noreia's grandmother reached into her basket again and gave her an oyster with a beautiful opalescent blue gray pearl inside. "Save this pearl, Noreia, for when hope is lost at sea. Then call Xiang's name as you hold onto the pearl. When you are in distress, look up to the skies above the ocean and say his name. There, you will notice him like a silver ribbon through the clouds. He can fan his wings to guide the fog. The fog will cloak you, so that your enemies won't find you. You will be safe!" Marcelina went on knitting.

When her eyes grew heavy, Noreia felt the effect of the long journey. "You've been kind to me. Can I do something for you?" she asked.

"Continue to be the good hearted girl you are, Noreia. Get some sleep now by the fire. You have a long journey ahead of you, yes?" Grandmother Marcelina kissed Noreia's forehead and tucked a handmade quilt around her granddaughter to keep out the cold. The bright quilt was patterned with squares of Irish linen, indigo cotton, and here and there patches of smooth silk. The quilt warmed and soothed her. She fell into a restful slumber.

Noreia awoke to her grandmother's voice. A gust of cold, damp wind stirred the blue, yellow, and green curtains. Out the window, the sun was below the horizon, just starting to rise. Small white sails were buoyant upon the dark water.

Kitchen plates were propped over the mantle. Her evening slippers were dry on the hearth.

"Noreia, you must hurry!" her grandmother said. "There is barely time left to sneak onto the ship before the crew awakens!" Noreia threw on her slippers and cloak and kissed her grandmother on the cheek.

"*Au revoir*," said Noreia. She unlatched the door and slipped into the dawn.

"*Bon chance*," her grandmother said.

Noreia took out the pearl her grandmother had given her. Then she put it back in her pocket and buttoned it securely. The sun was still hiding beneath the sky. She had to get to the ship before the guards found her.

Over the sand in plunging steps, she sped toward the great warship. She passed two fishermen talking as they mended their nets.

"A dragon is a frightful creature!" said one. "My brother was taken away by one, and no one ever saw him again. When his boat brushed ashore, the boards were broken to splinters!"

The other fisherman gestured to the trees beyond the sand. The morning wind caught up the dry grasses where he pointed.

"At night, you might hear the swoosh and cry of dragons flying over the forest. There, over the dunes," said the eldest fisherman.

Noreia ran on, worried by their gossip.

In the near distance, she saw the unmistakable carved prow of the king's ship, anchored by the dock. Its silhouette was dark against the sunrise, inspiring Noreia to think of her quest.

She seized her chance. She pulled off her slippers and leapt across the gravel and sand as foamy, cold seawater washed over her feet.

As she ran on beside the ascending sun, Noreia imagined gentle dragons living in peace among ferns, exotic flowers, and waterfalls. She would be glad when the fairies welcomed her.

Noreia groaned and stopped, only a few yards from the boat dock. What was she doing, leaving her family behind, and all the people she knew? She looked back at Grandmother's cottage and felt her strength renewed. Her feet found their way, first one foot and then the other. She broke into a sprint, staying near the water's edge. Her bare feet slapped against the cold sand.

Soldiers were already boarding the ship over the gangplank from the dock. Sailors were trimming the sails, as the early sun bathed them in gold.

CHAPTER 13
The Journey Begins

Seagulls called. The crewmen were already at work. Some were polishing the railings, while others mopped the deck with buckets of seawater. Noreia had no time to waste. She waited until no one was looking, then crept onto the lower deck of the ship. She slipped behind a barrel, hiding among the cargo in a splintery wooden crate. She curled up under her dark wool cloak, excited and nervous.

She counted the days she had been gone from her parents. Yesterday was her birthday, which meant that today was March third, the day the royal ship would sail for Dragonera Island. She thought about the length of the journey. Would it take a month...or more?

Several men were lifting crates onto the creaking deck when the captain, in a Navy blue coat with brass buttons, came up to them.

"The princess is missing again," said the captain. "His Majesty has decided to stop the expedition until she is found."

"How terrible!" said a young sailor wearing a striped shirt and a dark beret, "If you ask me, that girl's just playing hide-and-seek."

"More attention is what she probably wants," said another.

"She was last seen at the party. Her birthday celebration ended unexpectedly yesterday evening when a thorough search of the castle failed to locate her," the captain told them.

"How can we help?" asked the young sailor.

"If a search party is needed to look for her, His Majesty is the one to decide. Certainly not any of our crew," said the captain.

Noreia sat in the shadows, watching the men ready the ship as the water rocked and lapped at the hull. Hearing the sound of royal trumpets, the sailors stopped short. What could this news be?

A beribboned messenger in striped hose strode along the dock, now crowded with people, and the fanfare ensued as the boyish fellow boarded the ship. The first mate read the dispatch from the castle messenger to his crew, who leaned forward to hear him.

"A royal decree has been issued. We believe that Princess Noreia is in the surrounding areas of Emerhill. By the queen's order, the king's expedition to Dragonera is hereby postponed! Until the princess is found safely, all sea expeditions excluding merchant vessels will remain in dock until further notice."

Noreia was stunned. Whatever would she do now? The huge ship shifted in the harbor. What could she do? If she remained hidden, the ship would never sail. If she revealed herself, her father would stop her journey to Dragonera.

A page with another scroll ran down the treacherous stone stairway to the dock. Breathless, he trotted down the splintery dock and onto the sailing vessel, where he handed his scroll to the messenger on the boat. The messenger unfurled the second scroll and read aloud. "The king's hunting expedition will set sail this morning as planned!" Cheers and applause came from the crewmen.

Noreia's eyes filled with tears of relief. She looked up from the slow motion of the water. High above her were the cliffs of Emerhill, where she had played as a child.

The crew went back to lifting barrels and wooden crates from the dock onto the ship with ropes and pulleys. Noreia caught sight of the wild geese that swam around the dark, murky water of the bay. Suddenly, there was a cry that made the crowd on shore disperse like silver fish in a stream.

"Make way! Make way for His Majesty the King!" Noreia saw the king's cloth banners cut through the throngs of people and heard his heralding trumpets playing a fanfare. The heads of passersby stretched over the multitudes to catch a glimpse of His Majesty, King Roparz. When Noreia caught a glimpse of him, she marveled at the sight of a person of such importance. She saw him not as her father. She saw him not as a king. He was a kingdom!

The king made an official announcement to the crowd. "My royal subjects and citizens of Emerhill Kingdom! This expedition to Dragonera Island is important to all of us. To those citizens wanting to know more about the various sea creatures living in our vicinity, the information gathered from this exploration will answer our questions, and no doubt raise some new ones. I remain your King Roparz I."

Noreia pulled the hood of her mantle tightly around her neck. As cold air seeped into her high collar, she was afraid the chill would freeze her. Her tears were warm against her cheeks. She lost herself for a moment, thinking of her mother. What was she doing, leaving her family behind? But her mission was unavoidable. She had to think of the dragon's family.

Down at the dock below the ship, multitudes of young mothers and infants cried. The sailors were waving their arms to their families. The royal guards pressed the crowd back. The ship was about to set sail.

CHAPTER 14

Across the Sea

"All hands! All hands! Set sail for Dragonera Isle! Pull up anchor! Trim the mainsail!" the captain shouted from the foremast.

Behind her, there was a mad swarm of activity. Sailors darted in all directions, some climbing the masts like squirrels. Others hauled up the mainsail. The great sheets fluttered and billowed aloft. The sun's glare flashed at her from between the sails and the rigging.

Several sailors dredged the mossy anchor from the water and hoisted it onto the deck.

"Ready, Captain!"

"Port!"

"Yes, Captain. Ready about!"

The enormous ship shifted like a leviathan into the eye of the wind and eased away from the mayhem of the dock. Nautical flags fluttered in the wind, along with Emerhill's colors. Masts tipped in the wind as the ship's mates yelled for order. Wisps of fog circled the hills of the mainland.

"Eye of the wind, due east!"

"Falling off! Head course southwest!" The captain stood at the helm, not glancing back.

Voluminous white sails luffed upon the square-rigged mast. As the great ship groaned like a sleeping giant, it pushed through the waves with full sails. Morning light caught the features of the wooden masthead, with its Celtic carvings. It was a fine merchant trade ship. Noreia's father was proud of it's agility. She was prized as a passenger ship and for its new lateen sails. These diagonal sails could be easily controlled amid the shifting winds of the Atlantic Ocean.

Noreia stayed hidden in her crate, in case a sailor might notice her walking on the deck. The ship was beyond Emerhill Bay and headed out into the Atlantic when she felt the first pang of fear. She was afraid of leaving her home, however strong she felt her reason was. Every noise frightened her. Only the sounds of seabirds were comforting, reminding her of the land she was leaving.

Even so, Noreia felt the strange excitement of the journey. In Emerhill, she belonged to her father, but if she could survive on Dragonera Isle, she would be claiming herself and her future.

She became used to the footsteps of the sailors. She dozed with one eye open, until drawn to the boisterous noise of sailors laughing. That night, she sneaked out of her crate while the crewmembers were below deck. She crept to the railing, but not too close. Although the stars were spread out like gems around the moon, they failed to distract her from her hunger. Drowsy with exhaustion, she fell asleep.

Noreia awakened an hour later to a familiar aroma of wine and gravy. She looked into a porthole that glowed with candlelight from the dining cabin. The men were eating at a round table lit by a hanging lantern. She could not make out what they said, but what they ate kept her imagination alive.

The sailors' dishes were filled with delectable vegetables and steaming potatoes covered with rich gravy. The scent of roasted beef, carrots, wine, and onion drifted through the air. A hint of garlic wafted from the galley to overwhelm her senses. King Roparz was seated at the captain's table. Noreia leaned in closer to listen.

"The princess must be found. We could look for her near the Bay of Biscay on one of these islands the map does not show," said the captain.

"What is your logic, Captain Collin?" asked the king. "My daughter is probably hiding somewhere in my own woods. Maybe she went to the village. She'll be safe and come home when she's tired of this little game of hers. She's just a child."

"She might have become lost in a small sailboat. Maybe we should search for her," said Captain Collin.

"She will be found close to the castle. I've left specific instructions on where to look for her with the royal guard. I'm confident that the plan will work."

"But Your Majesty!"

"You are not listening to me, Captain Collin! My wife believes the worst, but I am optimistic that she shall be found near the palace. I know my daughter well, and she only wants to bring my expedition to a halt," said the king.

"I hope you're right, Father," said Prince Dalwyn, eating a forkful of potatoes. "She has a wild spirit. Who can guess where she might have wandered?" Dalwyn added as he reached for the salt. The brass lantern swayed with the movement of the ship.

"I've had enough of your remarks, Dalwyn! We shall reach the island in a month's time. We will comb the island until every dragon is discovered. I'll build another dungeon for them there if necessary. My kingdom must be safe from the dragons. The townspeople are truly frightened. The dragons dare breathe fire and attack men in my kingdom? Never again shall dragons cause my people to live in fear. Full speed ahead!" The king resumed cutting his food and eating.

The prince whispered something into His Majesty's ear as the cook served him more gravy. King Roparz stopped chewing and put down his fork.

Ominous clouds loomed over Noreia as her mind turned in somersaults. Would Father and Dalwyn capture every dragon on the island? The dragons! How could they be safe?

The princess opened her small brocaded pouch by pulling the strings. She took out a small leather bound volume, the one her brother had chosen for her from their father's library. Her survival book! She opened it once again and felt its pages between her fingers. She turned to the contents page carefully.

"A Shipwreck Manual" Noreia read. "Chapter One: Identifying Survival Needs; Chapter Two: Tools for Survival; Chapter Three: Survival in Different Terrain; Chapter Four: Survival with Animals." She soon fell asleep.

CHAPTER 15
The Storm

The sea went on forever. The horizon line was sometimes just a blur between the sky and the sea. Some days, she could not see through the fog. Other days, she slept.

The days were monotonous, but Noreia kept track of how long she had been aboard with a piece of rock. She made a small mark upon the crate for each sunrise she witnessed. It had been a fortnight since Noreia had boarded the ship in Emerhill. Now it was May 14th.

Noreia was resourceful. She had watched the cook take his mug of beer and plate of bread out on the deck at the stern of the boat. After downing the beer and half the bread, he always strolled back to his cabin, leaving his plate on top of one of the crates. Noreia noticed that the beer often made him forget about both the plate and a water jug, leaving her some scraps of bread and enough water. Sometimes she found a piece of fish as well.

One morning, the water was strangely calm. Noreia looked across the sky as clouds covered the horizon. The wind picked up, and Noreia glimpsed the ship's sails fluttering and flapping. Sailors grabbed for the rigging.

Leeward tack!" yelled the captain. The great wooden boat

creaked and groaned like an old hinge. "Falling off!" Sails rippled and the Emerhill flag quivered and waved.

While several sailors rushed and stumbled, others were tying down the ropes. Noreia moved out of sight, looking around the side of the cabin near the stern. The mist and spray of waves spattered her neck. A wave curved over the railing and slapped against the deck. Her teeth chattered. She trembled with fear even more than from the cold. The mast moved back and forth, which caused her a combination of nausea and panic. Metal chains dragged against the deck.

That night, the water became calmer, yet not still. The boat was jittery, the way a knight's horse becomes nervous before battle. Dark gray clouds obscured clusters of stars, and the wind withheld. Noreia was terrified.

Droplets of water sprinkled her hair. They slid over her face and neck. Raindrops scattered over the deck, gaining in rhythm and strength. The rain pattered and made puddles on the smooth wooden deck. Creeping from her hiding place, the princess slid across the deck. Gripping the railing, she pulled herself up. She saw her brother Dalwyn, from a great distance, at the helm of the ship. He had grabbed hold of the wheel to help the captain steer.

Lightning bolts lit the black sky in sudden sparks. The ship rolled and tipped. Waves sprayed the sailors who were hauling in the mainsail and tying down the other sails. Noreia clung to the railing to keep from falling and being washed off the deck. She hung on when the rain pummeled the wooden planks beneath her.

She grabbed the rope ladder as it swung from the mainstay and tied herself to the mast with the loose end of a rope. Clinging to the mast, Noreia raised her head. With-in the clouds, a shining silver gray dragon slipped through the fog. He was magnificent, his great wings fanning the whitened fog toward the boat like a dancer. His movements brought him closer, while the fog grew thicker. Xiang! Noreia could no longer see the deck at her feet. The ship rocked, water sloshing at her shoes. The Mainyard creaked overhead.

Foreboding gray clouds descended like shadows falling to the front deck. No, it was giant birds, as big as a man, with curved talons and strong, feathered wings. "Rocs," Noreia whispered to herself.

The birds of legend were after them. Noreia had heard they lived only in the ruins of fortresses and old castles. She had thought they were extinct.

With their large beaks, the Rocs wrenched the sailors away from the rigging and rope ladders. Off they flew, only to give way to more birds. These lifted the decorated of-ficers, screaming, from the bow of the boat. The wind muffled Noreia's own screams.

She freed herself from the mast, fell, and pulled herself upright again. A wave leapt over the side of the ship, and she struggled to maintain her balance.

When her father drew his sword to fend off a giant Roc, she caught a good glimpse of the creature. It had gray feathers and a sharp beak like a hawk's. Its eyes were snake-like and sinister. King Roparz 's sword appeared to be no match for the beast. Dalwyn thrust his sword at it, too, only to see it fall, clatter, and slide across the deck. The Roc flew at the king, its jaws snapping, talons raised. The king was thrown against the railing as he swiped his sword at the horrible bird. With a single stroke, the Roc lay upon the deck, a crumpled mass of feathers.

Noreia dared not approach the bird, fearing it might be alive and ready to defend itself. Dalwyn went to examine the bird, turning it over cautiously with the point of his sword. The bird lay still. For a moment, a sense of calm came to Noreia's mind.

The bird raised its head just as Dalwyn turned his back. With its claws out, it rose in the air like the roar of a fire from a single ember. It grabbed the prince by his shoulders, tearing through the darkness with a screeching cry. Another, even larger bird threw itself onto the deck. It tore the weapon from the king's hand as if it were a small twig.

Noreia ran forward as the huge bird of prey snapped at the king with its frightening beak. As her father rose up into the jaws of the Roc, Noreia picked up a heavy crate and hurled it at the bird. She found the courage to grab hold of its tail, only to have it slip through her fingers when the bird scratched her arm with its talons. The Roc flew away with King Roparz struggling in midair. Noreia peered over the liquid waves and up into the terrible dark above.

Just then, the boom of a sail swung toward her and knocked her to the boards. Her head spun in time with the waves. Her body felt light, as if it were floating in the air. With her last remaining strength, she crawled to the safety of her hiding place.

CHAPTER 16

Gannet

Light flickered and flashed onto Noreia's face as morning sun beamed through the wooden slats in the crate where she lay. She rubbed her eyes, sat up, and looked around.

She looked over the side of the ship, now anchored amid a beautiful inlet. The sand was a brilliant white and the sea was a rich teal blue. The rails of the ship were broken, and many of the sails were in tatters. Even the hull of the boat was damaged by a large hole. There was a break in one of the masts, probably from the impact of the ship when it hit the rocks. Her mind reviewed the moment the birds had attacked, and left their mark on this once majestic ship.

There was a strange quiet again. The crew was not on deck, and she felt a sudden fear of being deserted. Noreia assumed they had gone to explore the island, looking for food.

A lone seagull's horrible screech cawed above her. He landed near her with a large piece of bread in his mouth. She reached, but in her weak condition, she only made a swatting gesture in the bird's direction. A few more seagulls descended, screeching as obnoxiously at the first one. Just when the noise was too much to bear, out of the clear azure sky sailed a beautiful, strange bird. The other seagulls dispersed in a flurry of gray and white feathers. The first seagull gave up the piece of bread and flew off.

Noreia thought she heard someone say, "Don't give up," but only the bird—a heron, with orange and black features on its face and brilliant blue eyes—stood there atop the wooden crate.

"What? Did you just say—? Who are you?"

"Pardon me, Mademoiselle, I am Gannet. May I be of assistance?"

"*Merci!*" said Noreia. The piece of bread was beside her.

"*Je vous en prie!*" said Gannet. "You're welcome."

"Are there dragons on this island? Is this Dragonera?"

"No, Mademoiselle."

"The ship must have landed on some other island, then, one where birds can talk. Wait, if you can speak, we must be—"

"On Fay Linn Island. Gannet here, at your service," said the bird.

Noreia took a bite of the bread. "Please help me find my father and brother. They've been stolen away from the ship by the Rocs!"

Gannet said, "The Rocs! You are in great danger, then. Follow me. Flap your wings, and off we—" Gannet flew off the deck of the ship and landed on a branch facing the island.

"I don't have any wings!" Noreia called after him.

"No problem! I'll ask some friends for help. Galena! Galena!"

A lovely woman emerged from the deep water. She had golden hair and wore a crown of carved coral, decorated with seawater pearls. Noreia reached her hand over the side for her, in a panic that the woman might drown. The woman laughed playfully and smiled at her.

"Do not be frightened! I am in no danger. I'm a mermaid."

A splendid mermaid she was, too. She flashed through the air as she flipped her tail out of the water. Then she dove back into the water like the swift arrow of an Emerhill archer.

"Can you help me?" asked Noreia.

"I can swim you to shore! Take my hand and off we go," said Galena.

Noreia backed away from the railing. "I'm afraid to swim here. The water is deep!"

"It's not difficult. I'll keep your head above water. Hold on."

Noreia and the mermaid swam through the deep sea until they reached the shore. It was a strange and beautiful place, but Noreia couldn't think of anything but finding her father. Would he still be alive, if the bird had left him alone?

"Who lives here?" Noreia asked. When she turned around, Galena had already swum from the shore.

Gannet caught an incoming breeze and flew out of sight.

The sand beneath Noreia's slippers was made of white marble dust. Her feet sank into its pearl like smoothness. She wanted to memorize the color of the water, a pale and greenish blue. She walked beside the frothy incoming tide until she found a trail through the forest. The path might lead her to her father and brother!

The trail ran straight ahead. Noreia headed into the trees, which grew like long staffs into the clouds above her. The ground was littered with leaves, and the smell of damp earth was in the air. After a while, she came to a rough-hewn stone bridge covered in ivy. A cypress had curled its branches around the railing, and moss covered its steps. Below the bridge was a channel where a river had been, now filled with growing silver beech trees and ferns.

There is a special place and time, deep in the ancient forest. For centuries, children have come to hide in quiet glades like the one Noreia had found. It is where knights and ladies are as close as the whispering air. Fairies live under every leaf, and their lives are touched and changed by the children. One child alone can bring an entire fairy village into existence.

When Noreia stopped and listened, she could hear the faint sound of laughter. It was childlike, high and full of joy. Then the wind died down and there was nothing but silence, except for the occasional fall of a maple leaf.

She ran up the steps and looked out over the stone bridge to survey the forest, then took in a breath and listened. When she closed her eyes, she heard what she thought was laughter again. It was the trickling water of a stream.

She picked up a maple leaf and turned it over in her hand. To her surprise, a tiny elfish fairy, the size of a small chess piece, was clinging with both hands to the edge. "No!" he cried. He dove off the bridge, and Noreia tried to catch him. "A giant!" he called out.

She listened in terror for the sound of the fairy hitting the leafy ground. Instead, she heard the magical roar of a lively river. She looked over the bridge in disbelief.

CHAPTER 17

Fay Linn Island

Fairies of every size were riding maple leaves down the rapids. The tallest fellows ran and jumped into the water from low branches. Then came rowers in walnut shell boats, whose respectable wives carried parasols made from Bougainvillea blooms.

"Hello!" Noreia said, pleased that the sun had come out. The day had the warmth of early spring, and the finches were preening their feathers.

"Look, Rozenn! Another giant. I hear they are friendly," said a tiny man, holding the hand of his tinier daughter by the side of the brook.

"I think she's friendly, Yannic," said a little fairy lady.

Noreia heard the sound of small reed flutes. Rolling down the brook came a carved gondola made from a hollowed tree branch. The fairies scrambled to take their places along the rocks. Then Noreia saw Rayenna, the fairy who had given her the fairy book and the green pearl. Now she was the same size as the little people beside the stream, yet even more mesmerizing. Her pearl crown and trailing robes sparkled like raindrops on the flat green leaves of a

rose. Her gondola was decorated with tuberoses, and a Glasswinged butterfly was pulling the boat.

"Voila! Welcome to my home," the little fairy said to Noreia.

"Wondrous!" said Noreia, taking a step back. "Fairies are as real and magical as the manual said they were. But I'm surprised to find you here." Along the riverbank, she noticed small cottages made of redwood bark. The yellow branches of the trees held round fairy dwellings lit by glowing magical crystals. "Do you know where I can find my father and brother? Where would the Rocs have taken them? I want to know if they are safe, please."

"I can tell you only that it will take all your love and

strength to bring them back," said the fairy. "Beware! The
Rocs have a strange power, the power to sway men's minds.
As we speak, General Nettlelurch and the Rocs are
searching for us."

"What if they find us? Will they harm you?" asked
Noreia.

"The Roc leader, Holocene, cannot harm us with
weapons, because we are invisible to him. He and his
general, Nettlelurch, do not believe in fairies!" And with
a final wave of her hand, the lady started to fade. The
fairies in the stream faded into autumn leaves, and the
walnut shell boats became impossible to discern from the
bark of the trees behind them. The laughter Noreia had
heard was farther away now. The green fairy Rayenna
and her descendants were vanishing before her eyes.

"Rayenna?" Noreia called. "How can I...?"

Rayenna reappeared, glowing as before. "Do you need
me?" asked the concerned fairy.

"How can I defeat the Rocs, Rayenna?" Noreia asked.

"You must step forward to face your enemy. Now is the
test, Noreia. You are a heroine!" Rayenna stood back, proud
and admiring.

"No, Rayenna, I'm not. I'm just a girl trying to find her
father and brother. I can't —"

"There are only three silver rules in Fairyland!" Rayenna
interrupted. "Follow your heart, never use the word *can't*,
and answer every question correctly. And one more spell.
Noreia, know that any creature, human, elf, or dragon, is

granted one wish at the gate of Fay Linn Castle. But they mustn't have broken more than one of the Silver Fairy Rules." Rayenna waved her wand, and a cascade of sparkling fairy dust fell upon Noreia's head.

"Follow my heart, yes, but how can I know how to answer each question?" asked Noreia.

"If you truly are a heroine, you'll know what to say!"

Noreia called out, "Rayenna, come back, where are you?"

Noreia caught her own mind drifting off. There she was, staring into the leaves from the deserted stone bridge. A great sadness came over her. Noreia felt awkward in the beauty of the woods without the fairies. She pulled Lisette's cloak around her and ran down the steps of the bridge. When she heard the songbirds around her, her spirit felt refreshed and alive. She opened the embroidered purse hidden in her cloak and pulled out the fairy book again. She read the beginning of the chapter about Fay Linn Island:

"*An old footbridge spans the Great River. It was once the entrance to the Silver Castle. The king and queen of Fay Linn reigned over the Realm of the Air until the day the wild Rocs attacked the castle.*"

As she read the paragraph, a chilling wind curled its way around her shoulders. Noreia's body quivered as a rush of fallen leaves moved past her into the trees. She heard the strange call of a Roc sweeping over the gentle stream. The bird moved like a ghost over her as she covered her head with her arms. Then it stole a seat near her, on a mossy wall of stone.

She could see castle ruins through the birch trees behind

him. The scruffy Roc tipped its head toward her and said, "We meet again, my Princess! My master will be pleased."

Noreia clutched her precious purse, pulling it closer. "Who are you? Where's my father and brother?" she demanded.

"Somewhere out of reach of pesky princesses asking questions. I'm Nettlelurch, general of the Roc army." Noreia moved to a safer distance from the menacing bird. "I will present you with a riddle you must solve. If your guess is incorrect, your brother and father will remain with me. You may have three guesses, Princess!"

Noreia took a deep breath. "What's the riddle, then?" she asked.

The Roc general began:

"Reminiscing, looking back,
As a sailor's tilting tack,
Who am I that won't return,
Lost in memory?"

Noreia was terrified, torn between her fear and the love of her family. She didn't dare to run away now. She had to solve the riddle, for the sake of her poor father and brother. "If I answer, then will you free them?"

"Maybe!" Nettlelurch replied with a snarl.

"Remembering, then looking back." Noreia paced the ground. "Who am I that doesn't return and is lost in memory? Is the answer, then, time?" The bird turned its head.

"No. You've forgotten that time never looks back. Two more tries, and soon your brother and father will say hello to the new king of the Fairy Realms, King Holocene."

"I've got it! The answer is *the past*!"

The horrible bird looked very satisfied. "No."

"No? But it makes sense," said Noreia, pacing again, "and I only have one more guess? What could it be, then?"

"It's somewhere very specific, and you won't ever guess the answer," said Nettlelurch, lifting his beak haughtily.

"Fay Linn Castle!" As she spoke, the bird became flustered, fidgeting on his perch.

"Why? What do you mean?" snapped Nettlelurch.

Noreia thought for a minute. Then she answered, "Because Fay Linn is only a memory now. It relied on the hopes of children who believed in the legacy of the Lore Kingdom. Reminiscing is how you get there, though the way may be indirect. It will take each of us to make Fay Linn more than an island!"

"Now you've done it! The Roc king will be furious with me! Now you may pass beyond this archway. However, you might find something else blocking your way!"

"What do you mean? By an enemy force? Tell me!"

The Roc flew away, leaving her question unanswered. Not knowing what to expect, Noreia followed the path through the trees to a fortress ruin, covered in ivy and peat moss. The fortress hid from the waking light. The place looked ancient and still. Cobwebs confirmed her theory, as did the vine of Bougainvillea that had long ago been part of the castle grounds. A large strawberry shrub covered the front of the castle.

A great waterfall was near the old silver brick castle. The drawbridge was still there, lowered in place. Noreia crossed the drawbridge, over a moat strewn with fallen orange red leaves, and walked through the main gate.

CHAPTER 18

The Silver Castle of Fay Linn

Noreia studied the mossy silver brick and marble walls, turning in multiple directions as if faced with a maze. She thought back to the times she and Argantael ran circles through the maze in their grandmother's garden. She remembered chasing each other to find the fountain. She always finished last.

Trees bent their branches with the burden of the wind. The warmth of midday had vanished, and the fog had moved in front of the sun. The air chilled her, and she clutched at her cape, shivering as gray clouds misted the ground.

She was aware of the Rocs circling above. Nettlelurch, their general, was perched upon a high wall of the ruined castle. The menacing creature watched her from the top of a decaying archway. He resembled an oversized crow, whose claws ended in big curved talons. His feathers were scruffy and unkempt, and his armor was rusted and scratched. He wore a helmet that hooded his fierce, staring eyes.

"So, would you like to free your relatives, Princess?" asked the Roc with a cackle.

"Yes! Of course, I'd do anything. What do you want from me?" Noreia said.

"Anything? That puts me in an interesting position, Princess! Then give me your father and brother to keep!"

"No. You must free them!" The cold wind pulled at her cape.

"It is not for me to decide," said General Nettlelurch. "According to tradition, persons who pass over this drawbridge must make a wish. You may have one wish granted. However, you may not return your wish to trade for a better one. Only one!" cackled the Roc general.

"He's awfully sure of himself!" Noreia whispered aloud. Crisp leaves spiraled through the air. "I wish—"

"That won't work! You've got to choose the wish you want from among the garden of wishing willows." Noreia looked around her, noticing that the overgrown grass around the castle was full of small wishing willows. Each of them had a small parchment tag attached.

Noreia kneeled down to read them.

"*Entitles the bearer to one wish. Without guidance, the bearer of this wish is given a chance to return from Fay Linn as though nothing out of the ordinary has happened.*"

Noreia read the ticket on a second willow. "*This wish, granted, allows the bearer to a year of ownership of a unicorn who now lives on Fay Linn.*" Noreia saw how wild the strange wildflower garden was. She read another tag.

"*The bearer will promptly be given the opportunity to spend a year in Fay Linn. Forget your problems and stay in Fay Linn, where gnomes, fairies, and legendary*—" Noreia stood up, walked back to a boulder, and sat down. She thought and thought. What one wish could ever undo her problem? The Rocs had her father and brother.

"I can't choose from these!" she cried. "None of them are what I would wish for."

"Aha! You broke a rule! Not just any rule, but a silver rule. Now you may not ever pass, because—"

"Overruled!" Noreia turned to see Rayenna standing behind her. "I rule over what is fair and not fair in this Fairy Realm. This particular traveler is entitled to pass through the gate!"

"That's unfair. She broke the rule by using the word *can't!*"

"She didn't have a chance to say what her wish would be. Noreia?"

"Yes, Fairy Rayenna."

"Noreia, you may choose another." The fairy gestured to the patch of flowers again. Noreia noticed that the garden was overgrown with wishing willows that had no tags on them. She hand picked one willow and held it up, admiring it.

"I wish that my brother Dalwyn will be released from the Rocs' snares!" said Noreia. And she blew on the willow.

"You see, Nettlelurch?" said Rayenna. "She listened to her heart. The golden rule is that any traveler encouraged to stray from her own good intentions is forgiven for breaking one fairy rule. She was still entitled to the wish. A whole garden of want weeds—what will they think of next?" As the great fairy waved her wand, she disappeared into the forest.

"Curses! Yes, now you may pass," said General Nettlelurch.

"Where is he?" Noreia demanded.

"Your father?" cackled the general. "Darter! Hostilius! Open the drawbridge, soldiers! You'll soon realize they are here of their own accord."

"You won't easily convince him to leave," said Darter.

"He likes it here!" said Hostilius with a sly smile.

"You tricked them! Tell me what they wished for! You must have told them you knew where I was!" Noreia shouted.

"As wishes go, he made a bad decision," said Nettlelurch.

"Dalwyn?" Noreia ran along the foyer wall to the left and turned at a juncture. She sped down a pathway filled with weeds and over grown ivy. Finally, Noreia saw her brother, tied up with sailors' rope, leaning against a wall of the castle. Panicking, she ran to his side. "Let's go, Dalwyn, before the Roc changes his mind!" urged the princess.

"Not before I take what is now mine. Where's my sword, bird?" said Dalwyn.

"Dalwyn, no," uttered Noreia, pulling at his sleeve. Her brother's hands were filled with pebbles, dirt, and straw, which he cradled as if they were fine jewels and treasures. "It's too dangerous to challenge them. I tried my best."

"Take whatever you want. You have not chosen wisely, Prince!" said General Nettlelurch.

Prince Dalwyn picked up his sword as soon as Darter tossed it to the ground.

"Dalwyn! What have they done to you?" cried Noreia, untying him.

Dalwyn rubbed his eyes. "They promised us that we would find you!" said the mesmerized prince, embracing his sister.

"Tell me...where's Father? What have they done with him?"

"They tied him up behind that stone wall," Dalwyn said.

"Father! Father, are you hurt?" Noreia called. She found the king sitting in a pile of straw in a walled corner, his fingers sifting the dirt and straw from the ground. His hair was tangled and covered in straw.

"Father, let's go!"

"I wanted to become a great ruler! I am the great ruler of the fairies now," mumbled the hypnotized King Roparz.

"What did you wish for, Father? Think quickly, please." Noreia's nimble fingers undid the knotted rope that held his arms. She took his arm gently, but he pulled back.

"I wished for treasures beyond my imagination!" said the king, rubbing his aching forehead. "Noreia, I've been tricked!"

"We've got to get out of these ruins, Father! Please take my hand. Please follow me, Father. There must be a way out of this castle."

When they made their way back to Prince Dalwyn, he was stunned and shaken. As he looked around, fear was in his eyes. "What am I doing here? We've got to get back to the ship!"

"Promise me, Dalwyn, that you will not tell Father I am on his ship. You owe me for saving your life. I beg you, Dalwyn!" Noreia whispered to her brother.

"I won't, on one condition," said Dalwyn. "That you tell me why you are on the ship in the first place. A ship is no place for a girl!"

"Fine. I.... No, I can't tell you."

"You want to save those dragons, don't you? I was sure you were sane, but now I'm not sure." Her eldest brother walked a few steps toward the trees. "Anyway, I'll make sure Father stays out of your way," he said to her. "I owe you a favor for saving me. Thank you."

"You're my sister, Noreia. Now hurry. Our crew must be wondering where we are!"

"Careful, Dalwyn, when handling delicate treasure!" said King Roparz, studying the straw in his wet hands.

"I'll get those devilish birds! I'll get them for humiliating Father!" said Dalwyn, sinking his forehead into his hands. "There must be a way!"

Noreia dove into the fairy manual. "Spells for mammals, fish, birds," she read aloud. "Birds! Ravens, spells to disband an assembly of...pheasants, pigeons, quail, rocs, swans. Rocs! Here is the spell!" Then she said the spell aloud, softly:

"Foul rocs leave your nest,
You are uninvited guests!
Greed and evil be arrest'
Dismiss your greedy flock of pests!"

Clouds roamed through the pale blue sky. At first, they

were ominous, covering the sun's warm glow. Wind whipped through the branches of the trees, forcing them to lose leaves. Rocs fluttered from behind the castle walls in all directions, frightened by a strange spirit. They dispersed into the clouds, flapping away as rain fell onto the castle. Noreia took her brother by the hand and led him back through the gates.

When Noreia looked up, the mysterious Rocs had fled. There was no sign of their inhabitance. The ruins of Fay Linn Castle, with its many missing walls and rubble, stood in the distance.

"Noreia, I'll lead Father the long way through the woods. Meanwhile, you can run to the ship by another path, in case he wakens from his trance and recognizes you."

"Thank you, Dalwyn."

With careful steps, Prince Dalwyn led the dazed King Roparz into the forest. Noreia sat on a log, waiting for her brother to lead their father out of sight. She breathed a heavy sigh of relief when they disappeared among the foliage.

CHAPTER 19
Setting Sail

The tall Emerhill ship stood ready at anchor. The hole in the bow was repaired, with a new addition: A carved wood mermaid decorated the bowsprit. The face of the maiden looked like Galena's. New turned wood railings surrounded the ship, and the deck was swept clean of debris.

The Emerhill banner was flying again, raised to the masthead for the next part of their voyage. There was a new set of pilings and a new dock, where the ship's fore-stays were fastened. Noreia looked up at the spinnaker that a fairy sailmaker must have repaired. In the bright sunlight, Noreia saw a series of fairies running over the masthead, silhouetted through the mainsail.

She sneaked onto the ship and arrived back in her crate before her father and brother. She carried with her a small piece of marble brick that had once been part of the Castle of Fay Linn. Hearing the clamor of voices from the beach, she threw her cloak over her head, hoping to remain unnoticed by the crewmembers.

"I've never seen my ship looking so grand!" said the captain, running across the dock.

"It must have been the work of the fairies, Ironsmith!" said one wide eyed sailor to another.

"Must be! I never knew the legend was true. The village women say the fairies live on this island, Captain!"

"Maybe!" said the captain, chuckling. "Look! Here is His Majesty at last!" The captain looked out to the beach, where Prince Dalwyn and King Roparz were approaching the ship.

As the two boarded the ship, he said, "I am delighted you are here, Your Majesty! We, I mean the crew, were—"

"Never mind the formalities, Captain!" said the king. "To Dragonera!"

"Up anchor, men!" shouted the captain, as the crewmen untied the forestays and jumped aboard.

"Feathering!"

"Aye, Captain!"

"Larboard, then close haul!"

As the ship left Fay Linn Island, Noreia clasped the bag with the fairy book at her hip. Something about the fairies brought her luck.

The next morning was the nineteenth of May. The sun was blinking from behind the clouds. Noreia was rudely awakened, when the cook's son looked into the storage crates behind the kitchen deckhouse.

"Up with you, sailor—what in the world? Why, you're the princess of Emerhill! Your father is looking for you, and he'd pay a pretty franc to see you alive again," the cabin boy said.

"Please. If you agree not to tell him, I'll tell you my secret, and why I'm running away," said Noreia.

"What's in it for me? No reward if I don't turn you in,"

the boy said.

"Please don't tell my father. I'll let you have my locket. This is a picture of Grandmother. It's one of my best possessions in the world," said Noreia.

"Keep it! What would I do with it, anyway? Are you hungry?" asked the cabin boy. Noreia nodded. "I'll bring you some food, then," said the boy.

As the weeks passed, Noreia and Rylan became friends. They exchanged stories about their adventures. Noreia talked about her life as a princess, while Rylan talked about being a cabin boy and cook's assistant. He grew up on this ship and had never lived ashore.

By the first of June, Noreia no longer felt alone, to fend for herself—not with Rylan around. Rylan made a little ritual of surprising Noreia with food from the galley set aside for the officers. Each day, he brought her a small taste of fresh fish or a stale baguette. Every evening, Noreia forgot her worries telling Rylan about the dragon for whom she had left her father's kingdom. She and Dalwyn, on the other hand, stayed far away from each other to keep their father from noticing Noreia.

Three more months flew by, and there was some despair among the sailors. On the afternoon of August 30th, Noreia overheard two sailors talking near her hiding place.

"Hey, Bernard," said a young man.

"What?" asked Bernard, who was staring out to sea as he leaned against the ship's railing. "Dragonera Island? *Non,*

I know not, but I have faith that the captain knows where he is going."

"You sure it's not a wild goose chase? Are we chasing a mirage in a desert we may not ever reach?" asked the first sailor.

"Let's agree to disagree, then," Bernard said. "What I know is there were things I've seen on this last island I've never seen before! Maybe it's just something I ate, but—I told you—I saw fairies repairing the ship!"

There were doubts in Noreia's mind as well. Dragonera could be found only on Emerhill's secret maps. What made the captain so sure he could find it? Each day, the crew prayed for the island's appearance in the distant fog.

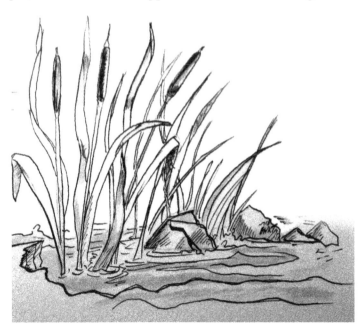

CHAPTER 20

Dragonera

"Land! Land ho!" It was dusk when Noreia awakened. A brass bell was clanging behind her. She pulled herself up in her crate, which was wedged between a couple of large sacks of grain and a few other supply crates. It was now September 1st!

In the half-light, a low curving form appeared in the distance.

"At last! The island is there!" a sailor yelled.

"A tropical paradise! I don't believe my eyes," cried another. The men threw their hats in the air, shouting and hugging each other. Noreia heard the mayhem, the scurry of heavy feet over the boards.

"All hands on deck! All soldiers on deck, men!" shouted the captain, standing near her father. The sailors hovered over the anchor as the captain ordered them to hoist it over the stern. "Drop anchor! Furl the sails!"

"Aye, Captain," said the sailors.

The soldiers stood in line for inspection as the captain cleared his throat to prepare an audience for the king. King Roparz had only to stand upon the upper deck to receive the attention of the sailors. They dropped their chores to look up at him.

"Men," said King Roparz, "I will explain the plan to you now. Bardwin, you shall take notes on my battle plan. I must have absolute cooperation as we proceed to embark on a discovery so compelling that it will change each of your lives! Together, here, we will capture and destroy the most destructive beasts of Dragonera, the dragons! As I read your names, remember your part in the battle plan.

"Worthington and Ironsmith, you shall scout the area in the forest beyond the beach. Report any evidence of dragons sighted there!"

The princess kept her place in the abandoned crate, well hidden behind the cabin on deck. She waited, holding onto her breath like a raincloud heavy with water.

"Yes, Your Majesty!" they replied.

The king motioned for the next three sailors to come forward. "You three will guard the beach with your arrows. Shoot to kill. Otherwise, the dragons may attack you first, as is their way. The rest of the soldiers—attention, men! Into the lifeboats, and all men ashore!"

When Noreia heard the boisterous crew moving again on deck, she pulled out the old sailor's uniform that Rylan had brought her and stuffed her hair in the cap. Using her cloak, she wrapped her belongings in a bundle, like the other sailors had done. She listened for the footfalls of the last crewmen carrying supplies onto the boats. As the last sailors piled into the last lifeboat, the princess slipped into the boat, too, unnoticed by the captain.

The boat was lowered into the water, and the oarsman rowed to shore. The sailors got out on the strange and exotic island, and when the rower set down his oars and stepped out of the boat, Noreia saw her chance.

She grabbed the oars and began rowing around the boulders and broken shoreline. Rushes rustled in the wind. Noreia dipped in the oars and pulled hard against the current.

"You, there! Sailor, stop!" the men shouted from the shore. Waves crested and fell, as Noreia pulled back as hard as she could. The bow lunged forward as she yanked the oars through the foaming water. She let out a sigh of relief as the rowboat slipped through the water, leaving the crewmen behind.

Water lapped against her boat, which rocked and shook with the current. It was beyond her physical strength to keep up her pace. She lifted the oars, listening, and thought of Xiang, lord of the fog.

Dragon lord, I call your name,
My boat awaits your wise command.
Ocean current, wild as flame,
The sea makes waves against the sand!

Noreia worried that she had asked for too much, yet her boat slid through the fog. The men's voices sounded far away from her then. Instead, she heard the calls of the thrush, the kingfisher, the firecrest, and the swift.

Soon, the princess found a small birch tree rooted by the rocks. She tied her boat to the tree trunk and hopped over its roots. She smiled, proud of the journey she had made. She pulled the boat onto the sand to save it from damage from the wild current.

The princess stood in amazement. She had arrived at Dragonera.

Noreia walked toward the leafy orange and purple birds of paradise that lined the path. She avoided the tiny sanderling footprints in the damp sand.

Palms rustled overhead as she ducked into the dark jungle. Entirely made up of the tallest of trees, it felt like a grand cathedral. The sun blinked through the canopy of palms. Lizards slithered around the boulders of the jungle ground. Even in the failing light of evening, she saw the bright colors of birds flash before her.

The jungle gave way to a stretch of sand and rocks that protruded from the bay like giant teeth. Eerie spiraling ferns and featherlike leaves lined the sand among waxy striped orchids. A chilling air surrounded her as she walked over the coral sand dunes back toward her father's ship. She planned to keep her distance, but she needed to know what her father was doing.

A short distance away, her father was inspecting his soldiers, standing at attention on the beach.

A furious dragon broke through the overgrowth of tropical vines. Her body was flexible, like a gigantic lizard's, and she had batlike wings. She looked at Noreia with a lost expression. Her jaws snapped at the assembled crew.

Noreia's father turned his head as the dragon approached the shore. With the instincts of a general, the king shouted without delay, "Ready, men, and—"

Noreia ran over the sand. The archers stepped into line,

loading their bows. Her father saw a ferocious dragon coming at them. Noreia saw a mother dragon defending her baby. "— fire!"

"Father, no-o-o!" Noreia shouted, running over the rocks toward the helpless dragon. Her cap fell away as she bolted toward her father's shining ship and glowing sails. Her feet trampled over the sand in small, plunging steps. Twenty archers released their bows at once from the upper deck. Sharp flints pierced the huge lizard's chest. Its mouth opened to catch a large breath. The immense dragon fell backward with a reverberating crunch of broken trees. Noreia ran toward it and fell to the sand.

As the advancing dragon shifted her head to look at the princess, the king ran toward his daughter.

"Noreia!" the king called, "My daughter—?"

Looking ahead, the king fell onto his knees. Noreia felt detached from him, as she leapt forward into the brush and vines of the jungle. The deeper the princess threw herself into the jungle, the more her heart ached. She had held to her own belief. The bond she had with her father unraveled in her hands like a rough and frayed rope. She couldn't let this gentle creature die.

Noreia found the dragon, wounded and bleeding, holding a mewling baby dragon gently in her claws. The mother was intimidating—five times the size of the mares her father kept in the stables. She had a long, elegant nose like a thoroughbred, though much narrower. Her teeth were sharp and long. She was covered with olive green scales.

Her large emerald eyes held the sadness of a thousand years. This creature, who minutes ago had frightened a king, cried out for her help.

Noreia crept beside the giant lizard's claws. And then, strangely enough, the dragon closed her eyes and groaned. The call was repeated in the distant hills. Noreia perceived that the mother dragon was crying out in pain, perhaps not only physical. Maybe she yearned for her help.

When the dragon mother opened her eyes again, she looked bravely at the small princess. It was a pleading look. She wanted urgent help for her child, a little green dragonling.

The princess slipped the infant from the desperate grasp of the mother's huge talons. Gathering the fledgling reptile in her arms, she rocked the baby, hoping it would go to sleep. The baby had a teal blue underbelly and wide amber eyes that looked into hers, studying them.

When Noreia glanced over her shoulder, she saw the flash of the soldiers' torches flickering in the wind. Under and over vines and fallen branches, they walked toward her.

"Your Highness!" Onward they came, thrashing at tree vines.

Noreia seized the moment. She set the dragon child upon her cape. She made a poultice from the moss and cooling leaves growing on the rocks nearby and gently rubbed it on the mother's wound. The mother was appreciative, and she made a satisfied groan. Their bond would last forever.

Like a hundred distant candles through the gnarled

branches, the soldiers' torches reappeared. "Princess Noreia! Make yourself known!" Prince Dalwyn called through the trees. "Noreia! Noreia!" Noreia was startled by her brother's voice, echoing through the jungle.

Before she knew what was happening, two large dragons appeared in the expanse of blue above her. Two armored golden dragons with translucent wings flew over her toward the beach. Fear struck her mind as the first one flew over. It was the Dragon Guard that Stalwart had told her about in Emerhill. The second dragon swooped onto a rock near her.

"I am Fogspell, messenger and scout of the Dragon Guard, who protect and defend dragonkind," he said. "I tell you because we have seen that you are helping Draighean, the wife of our leader. You have rescued the dragon child! I must inform you of an imminent danger of attack from our forces!"

"I mean you no harm. My father is sending soldiers. You must be careful!" said Noreia.

As the dragon turned to take off into the sky, Noreia thought of her father. What would happen to him if the dragons reached him?

"Wait!" she screamed. Fogspell was still. "My father doesn't understand. He will never have the ability to defeat the dragons. And his soldiers are unequipped to defend themselves. Please reconsider, if you think well of me."

"Noreia, we must not delay! Your father has attacked one of us, and we are bound to defend our slain dragon queen!" Fogspell did not wait for a reply, but bolted into the sky, shadowed by his scouts.

Noreia heard the terrible moan of the dragon lying before her. She was face to face with the mother dragon's huge wounded carcass and shriveled wings. She pressed her ear against the dragon's chest. Noreia's own heart was pounding. How could she save her, or was it too late?

She saw the mother dragon draw her final breath. At that very moment, the little reptile made a strange cry. His beak-like jaws opened and closed. He craned his neck to examine her face. Noreia looked into the baby's brilliant teal blue eyes. He tipped his head to one side, curious, not under-standing what had just happened.

It was an instinctive act, to save a dragon's child. Noreia scooped up the dragonling again and held it in her arms. She stumbled into the jungle to avoid the soldiers. She pushed herself through the feathery fronds of ferns and short palms. She climbed the rocky terrain, hoping it was safe to look back. The king's ship looked small through the branches of a short palm. She hid in the hollow of a large banyan tree, surrounded by thin trunks sprouting up from its roots.

The blood red sun sank slowly beneath the trees. The air was oppressive and moist, even during the cooler evening. She wept over the small infant, the lizard like being resting in her arms. She clasped him close to her, whispering, "Dear Divinity, thank you for this gift," and her eyes teared until the little reptile was a green blur in her arms.

Men from the ship tromped through the underbrush,

whacking at the tendrils of climbing vines. All night, the sailors searched for her. The flaming orbs of their torches flashed through the dense forest.

When the men stopped coming toward them and the torchlights had gone, Noreia decided that in the morning she would go find her father at the ship. She had to warn him of the dragons' plan to attack. Noreia clung to the fragile dragon in her hiding place. The dragonling looked up at Noreia with wide eyes.

CHAPTER 21

The Light of Day

Wild cormorants dried their wings near the shore, waiting for the sun's heat to break through the clouds. The small reptile was sleeping in Noreia's arms. She had spent the night curled up in the hollow of their immense tree. The soldiers had retreated, empty handed.

"I know, little one. We'll find a place for you. I'll take care of you, but first I have to convince my father to retreat." She smiled, imagining her mother's expression. What would she say to her, if she knew about the creature she had saved?

Noreia hugged the lizard to her and kissed his little head between the round eyes, blinking and searching her face.

Noreia wrapped her wool mantle around the infant lizard. She would go to her father directly. He would have to listen. Noreia hooked the bag onto her belt. Her feet felt numb inside her sopping velvet shoes. She would soon be warmer, from walking up the beach under the sun.

By the time they reached the king's tent, Noreia noticed that her shoes were dry. She stepped over fallen bits of bark and leaves. Boulders and ice plants bordered the sand where the royal tents stood set up along the beach. The reptile was crying.

Noreia could hear voices in front of the tents. The captain and King Roparz sat outside on wooden folding chairs, huddled over their campaign maps.

"To me, she is merely a malcontent. She is ungrateful and unworthy of the name daughter!" bellowed the king.

"But, Your Majesty must listen to reason. She has followed her conscience. She had led with the intention of her heart. Please reconsider, Your Majesty."

King Roparz looked thoughtful as he glanced up at the captain. "I am sick with worry. I would give anything to see her here alive. We have searched the jungle for hours! If only she weren't so presumptuous! She is strong willed, that one. I must know she is safe." Noreia's father looked out to sea. It was a calm day upon the water. The expanse of sky above them was full of lazy clouds.

Noreia advanced nimbly over the rocks and ran over the sand to the tents. She saw the startled captain's expression and her father's outstretched arms.

"Are you safe? Here and alive! We must find you food. You need water. Here, take some from this pitcher," said her father.

"Father, I'm here to ask for help," Noreia said.

"Why did you leave me, daughter? You sneaked onto my ship and completely disobeyed my orders!" said the king.

"We don't see the world the same way, Father. You must listen. Please understand me."

"Bring me cider and cheese. The finest only! Fruit, galettes, and—" he turned his head to his daughter, "whatever you want to eat, you shall have. My sweet daughter has returned to me!"

"Father. I need to tell you something. Something important," said Noreia.

"Whatever you wish!" answered the king.

"I don't want you to fight the dragons' army! You have no idea of their strength and power!"

"Noreia, you are intolerable! Don't meddle in what you don't understand."

"Retreat, Father, while you still can," Noreia said. "Your soldiers' lives are at stake. You have killed the dragon queen!" There was a strange silence. She dared to steal a glance at him. "And let me take the baby dragon back to our kingdom. He needs to be cared for, Father. Without his mother, he will not survive alone in this jungle!"

"Noreia, what would become of a dragon in Emerhill? He would attack the villagers! Be sensible with your wish, daughter!" A worried look crossed the king's face. "Return to us, Daughter, alone! Noreia, your mother misses you. You do not belong here any more than that dragon belongs with us," said the king. He got up and strode away from her on the shore.

"I will go with you only if you let the dragon come, too! Now he is part of me. How can I leave him to die?" the princess called to her father.

"You are a disappointment to me! You are a royal princess. Why must you defy me? Why on earth?" The girl ran after him. He turned his back and walked away.

"Because I care! I heard the testimonies of the fishermen and villagers! They were careless and selfish to blame a creature at peace!" Noreia ran after her father, who didn't turn to look back as he neared the ship. "Now there's going to be a war with the dragons unless you leave!"

"Noreia, please. Let's not discuss this further," said her father. He didn't glance back to look at her.

"If you want, I will not mention the dragon to you again. Let me live here to protect my friends. I will stay here until the baby dragon grows up enough to live on his own. But I'll need your help, Father. I need provisions from you for a month, after which your ship could bring servants and food so that we will survive."

King Roparz still did not turn to face her. "Noreia, you shall have the provisions you need. As soon as I reach Emerhill, I will send another ship filled with food and supplies."

"Father, look at me, please!" He kept walking until he boarded the ship. Noreia knew she would barely survive on the island.

She heard her father talking to one of his men. "I must trust that my daughter will survive here. Give her these arrows, along with my quiver to carry them. She may need to defend herself on this island. Tell the men on deck to make the preparations for battle."

CHAPTER 22
The Battle

The next day on Dragonera, Noreia ran to the edge of the forest with the dragon in her arms. She found a place among the tall ferns where she could spy on her father, standing on the dock with the captain. She made a small nest for the infant out of twigs filled with fine grasses. She covered him with ferns to keep him out of the sun.

Noreia was frantic, thinking of nagging questions. Why was her father so stubborn, and what could he possibly gain from fighting the dragons? Some of the male dragons were as big as a ship and wore full armor. Why would her father lead his army to a death sentence?

Knowing she couldn't change his mind, the princess consoled herself that her father would, at least, send supplies to help her raise the dragonling. She would stay on the island until the dragon was full grown and could survive on his own.

"Your Majesty," said the captain as the soldiers stood at attention awaiting morning inspection, "it is my duty to set sail for Emerhill Kingdom. The men are aware of the imminent danger on the island. They fear for their lives, because of the reality of facing the dragons!"

"Do they? We will not accept defeat, men!" the king said. "There is little to be gained from what a soldier does not attempt in battle. There is nothing to be gained from a man who retreats at the first sign of danger! We have the finest trained soldiers and the best fletchers and swordsmiths. We have cannons and weaponry at our disposal. The dragons have only primitive instincts and no strategy. Our tactic shall be to have archers at the ready on three sides of the beach. Ironsmith!"

"Yes, Your Majesty!"

"You will man the cannons! The men I will now name shall be posted at each end of the beach! Halterman! Weriwyth! Waltercroft! On board will be the archers from yesterday's encounter. My best archers will lead the rest of you in when to fire."

When a terrible noise began, Noreia recognized the sound. It was the vibration of dragon wings! She wanted

to shout, to stop her father, or to run onto the beach. Then she saw the little eyes staring up at her.

The hum became louder, as the Dragon Guard pushed through the clouds above the hills behind her. Winging through the sky, they wore iron chainmail. The dragon who led them was the most impressive in size and wingspan. They soared in formation over her head.

Noreia saw them head for the beach just before the arrows were released, a sound she would never forget. A wounded dragon fell helplessly out of the sky, crushing the soldiers underneath him.

Seeing the soldiers nocking their arrows, the dragon army flapped their great wings at full force. Down they flew at the soldiers, tearing the men's bows away in their jaws. Some of the soldiers were picked up and dropped from great heights, while the dragons' claws struck down many others.

The soldiers fired again and again at their foes, striking the tough lizard skin like a driving rain. Noreia screamed, but could not hear her voice over the battle cries.

It was not long before the frantic soldiers left the beach, dropping their bows and quivers, their daggers, and even their helmets. Swords clattered upon the ground. They hit the deck in their heavy armor, fending off the dragons that came close to the ship.

"Cowards!" screamed the king, holding his ground. But then, as the dragons descended, he dropped his long sword and ran for his ship, too.

CHAPTER 23
Survival

As her father's ship disappeared beyond the haze, Noreia stared out to sea. She held back her tears. She was alone.

Two distant birds were winging over the lagoon. She had seen them each day, circling the island. When she heard a noise, she would steady her stance and aim a single arrow toward the source of the disturbance. Fearing that the Rocs had come for her at last, she hid behind a tree to protect herself. She laughed aloud at her fears when they turned out to be noisy seagulls.

Noreia thought about the distance she had traveled from her kingdom to the island. She contemplated the fathoms of the sea itself. How would her brother and father tell the story of the Battle of Dragonera? How an army of ferocious dragons dared to attack him, a soldier and a king?

It was September 5th, the beginning of her fifth day on the island. She knew she needed to find food and water for the baby dragon, as well as for herself. Argantael had taught her how to spear a fish. She remembered the engravings he had shown her in a book. She had forgotten the title, and wished she remembered more. She hung her cloak upon the limb of a tree. She made a spear handle out of a fallen tree branch that she tied with dry reeds. Then, she searched for strong branches and small rocks. She created a spear point from a fallen arrow. She cut more string with a rock and wound the spearhead onto the branch.

Noreia waded into the shallow lagoon surrounding the island with turquoise water, reflecting the sky. Tall reeds and lily pads mingled between the rocks. The fish shone like silver in the sparkling sun. She found fishing with only a spear difficult, but eventually she succeeded in spearing a medium size fish. After using dry grass and a couple of sharp flints to make a fire, she brought the fish to her campfire. It was charred and bony compared to the fine trout with lemon and butter sauce she ate at the castle, but she was grateful to no longer be starving. She gave most of the fish to the young dragon, who made a terrible cry for more.

After she speared two more fish, she decided she needed a better system for catching them. This time, when she waded among the reeds and rocks, she dipped the silk rope veil from her hair into the shining water, pulling and gathering until a school of bright fish swirled and leaped from the makeshift net. She emptied them onto the rocks. The baby dragon gobbled up the creatures like chewy confections.

After a week had slipped by, the small dragon still didn't have a name. Noreia thought hard for a minute, staring out to sea. A light shone through the trees like a window or a door, and a memory surfaced, of an old fishing boat that had sunk offshore. She had found the ruined boat when she and Argantael were playing on the sand. The name written upon the bow was *Dormach*, an old Celtic word meaning "door to the sea." She had found the perfect name for the little dragon.

When he grew to be mature, Dormach would protect and defend her. When Dormach grew to his full height and had learned to fly, they would fly back to join her family. She still believed her father would be proud of her. She missed her mother.

The tree hollow was adequate to shelter them for another week or two, but soon she would need to build a cottage, where they would be safe from the elements and unfriendly sea creatures. Once two weeks on the island were spent, she scouted an area beyond the trees where the forest ended in a flat, rocky place, high above the western side of the island. There, she could see over the forest to the beach and a stretch along the water's edge.

It was a considerable walk through the forest to get there. The sun shone its dull heat upon the ground. The surface was hot enough to be uncomfortable to walk upon, even in velvet slippers. Noreia had an idea for a dwelling strong enough to withstand the tide and wind. She thought that the structure could be built of hand laid rocks.

By the beginning of the third week, the dragon could no longer fit in her arms. He was learning to stand. During that week, Noreia gathered the strongest branches she could find and applied a mud coating over them. Where she entwined two trees, she tied the first corner of the dwelling. The floor was laid with tied branches strong enough to walk on. It was covered with leaves and moss. She made the walls in the same way, except that she used gathered grasses to insulate the house from the wind.She lay thin, leafy branches over the walls to form a roof, adding tree bark to shade the two survivors from the relentless heat. She used tall grasses to tie the branches. She used palm fronds to keep the dwelling cool. She used pieces of sailcloth from an old splintered boat that had washed ashore to cover the windows. This made their new home pleasant.

It was a suitable shelter for the two of them. Dormach slept outside in his handmade nest, while the princess stayed inside the cottage, covered by her cape. Noreia often slept with one eye open, afraid that the Rocs might make a surprise attack. She used her father's quiver as a pillow, to avoid falling asleep. Her brothers had taken archery lessons from their tutors, and Noreia used to practice at the target when it was not in use. Her father had started her with a few pointers, although her brothers claimed she would never need the skill.

On the morning of September 22, Dormach became restless. Noreia pulled the sailcloth aside to let the sun shine through the window. She walked out onto the flatland overlooking the rocky cliffs, covered densely with tropical plants. Dormach was flapping his wings and hopping in slow circles. His web like wings lifted him off the ground for a second, and then he fell over onto his side. Frustrated but determined, he scrambled to his feet to try again.

Noreia was proud of Dormach and of their new home. She was proud that she had stood up to her father, and proud to have survived a month on Dragonera Island.

CHAPTER 24

The Dragon Guard

On the twenty-ninth day, there was a sound of wings in the air. Noreia knew who was making the sound when dragons appeared among the wind swept clouds. She feared for the life of the baby.

One came close enough to watch her from atop a pointed boulder. She supposed, in his polished golden armor and red plumed helmet, that he was a grand general. Noreia called out to Dormach, who simply stood a step in front of her.

The visiting dragon's eyes regarded her kindly. He tipped his head to one side as if deciding something. As they looked at each other, Noreia felt the unguarded acceptance she was seeking.

Then the general spoke. "I want to thank you," he began. "You have helped dragonkind. Please know that we do not fear you. I know you have shown much bravery in risking your life to save one of our fellows. You may call upon us whenever you are threatened. I am General Westwyn, at your service!" The other dragons slowly came forward as far as a nearby cliff.

"Thank you. We will need your protection." Noreia's shoulders relaxed. "Dormach is the name I have given to the little dragon."

"We have seen how you have helped raise the infant of Draighean, wife of Stalwart. He is our leader."

"Stalwart was my friend. I am Noreia, daughter to King Roparz. I knew him when he found shelter in a cave near my home. My father's soldiers shot him. He is slain now. His death was heroic. He was a friend!"

"You say you are friend, not foe. Why didn't you save him, or speak to defend him?" asked the general.

Noreia held in her tears. "I did try, but I failed him. He was gathering seaweed off the shore of my kingdom, Emerhill, when a royal ship went down in a storm. Believing the dragons caused the shipwreck, my father's men injured him, and threw him into a dungeon. He died beside me, because I was too late."

"I grieve for the loss of my king. You were kind to him, and we will return the care."

The next evening, when the sun painted the sky, Noreia asked Dormach to watch their home while she gathered firewood.

"Noreia, do not carry the wood yourself. I am bigger and stronger, and capable of carrying large branches for the fire tonight. Let me go, so that you can rest."

"Thank you, Dormach. You are thoughtful," said Noreia.

Dormach gathered enough firewood for a great campfire. General Fogspell and his lieutenants joined them. Fogspell asked if he could bring some of the fairy folk and elves to the campfire, and Noreia readily agreed. That first night, she told them of the arrival of a great ship that might come to rescue her, bringing supplies and perhaps taking her back to Emerhill. This brought about much excitement and revelry. A renewed strength and purpose came over her. Her father would send the ship as he had promised.

CHAPTER 25

On the Horizon

Days and nights followed, filled with stories of fairy kingdoms of long ago. Soon it became a tradition to gather each night around the fire to tell stories of their lives. Each day, Dormach became stronger, and better able to fend for himself. He ventured further out into the wood to explore. Each night, Dormach gathered enough wood for a fine, warming campfire. Surrounded by friends, he listened to the legends.

The forest dwellers rounded up their kin to sleep nearby, in the crook of a tree branch or inside a nest left behind by the egrets. They found several ways to set up swings on the branches of the banyans, where the little ones could look out over the storytellers who walked around the fire, telling stories at night.

On one such October night, when the stars were scattered around the moon, Alvar, the elfin general, was explaining how the Great Storm had changed their way of life.

"Once, what you see on this island belonged to the magical realm," said Alvar. The fairies' eyes grew bigger.

"What kind of magical realm, Your Highness?" asked a young fairy.

"It was part of the Realm of the Sea," said Alvar. "This was long before any of us were born, in an age when the dragons protected each magical spirit. Sprites, pixies, and elves lived here, and fairies!"

"How different is it now?" asked Noreia.

"Many of our families have fled to the fairy island of Lismoire, ruled by King Arne and Queen Perizada. They rule there today," said a fairy mother.

"The dragons put up a fight then, but eventually many fled, looking for other places to settle."

"What could frighten a huge dragon?" asked Noreia, leaning forward.

"A terrible force must have frightened them," Dormach said.

"When the Great Storm rained upon these shores, the Rocs seized their chance!" said General Westwyn. "That day, they planned to frighten away the fairies without warning. We succeeded in defending the fairy folk from the Rocs. We saved the Castle of Dragonera, but we left Fay Linn Castle undefended."

"Was that when Nettlelurch commandeered Fay Linn Castle?" asked a dragon soldier. "Were many of our magic folk killed during the siege?"

"Yes. The Rocs swept in and seized the castle, and the elder dragons used their fog to cloak the fairies, just under the trees. The Elfin Guard are the warriors who protect the merfolk, fairies, and dragons from harm today."

"I don't know where the fairies first came from," said

Noreia. "A book said that they came from the island of Fay Linn."

The various beings around the fire exchanged glances. The elfin warriors, leaning against their spears, looked up to the fairy folk with their glowing wings. They, in turn, looked out at the mermen, who watched from the sea. The voice of a small forest gnome broke the silence.

"Many of you know me," said the small, spectacled gnome. "I am Narthor, guardian of the forests of the Fairy Realms. I remember Fay Linn when Queen Marcelina and King Roran ruled. Their silver forest thrived with magical pears and peaches. After the Rocs attacked Fay Linn Castle, all that was left was ruins."

Then Dormach had a question. "What happened to the ruling dragons, General, and to the other dragons left on Dragonera?" Everyone turned to him.

General Alvar, the elfin leader, stood up to speak. "The dragons and Dragonera sea creatures thrived in your parents' kingdom, Dormach. The dragons ruled this island without fear of the Rocs. Now we must hide among the leaves to avoid them!"

"They circle over our island each day, looking for a weakness in our position!" said Adalbert, a dragoon and navigator for the Elfin Infantry. "They seek the most vulnerable of us, the sick, the youth, and the elders of our clan."

"I remember the songbirds who basked in the sun-light when the wise dragon, King Stalwart, and his queen,

Draighean, protected the fairies," said a young fairy.

"What happened to our benevolent king and queen who ruled this island?" asked a young elf from the trees.

Noreia lifted her head. "I tried to prevent their deaths," she explained sadly, "but my father and his men killed them both." There was a murmur in the crowd as the fairies and other beings discussed this terrible news. "There was a storm near my home as well. The storm led the people of Emerhill to believe that a dragon had attacked an Emerhill ship. That dragon was King Stalwart."

The fairies gasped in astonishment.

"And Queen Draighean? How did she die?" asked Dormach.

"She died defending her son, Dormach, right here on the beach."

Dormach turned away for a moment. Then he caught Noreia's eye. "One day, I will defeat the Rocs, General!" he offered. "When I am confident of my wings, I will drive the Rocs away!"

The fairies, the dragons, and the creatures of the sea cheered him. Then they looked at Noreia, to hear what she would say.

"I hope you are correct, Dormach. I certainly do," she said. "One day, you may rule this island as your parents once did. You will make me proud."

CHAPTER 26
Spreading Wings

The weather became cool, and the winter months introduced light, tropical rains. The rains worried Noreia, who expected storms to occur. She began to miss the cold winter months spent at Emerhill with her family.

The dragon continued to grow. During that tropical December, Noreia tutored him. She taught him to dodge arrows and to fish in the ocean. In the sun, they practiced flying. Day after day, Noreia placed him on a low hill, where he sprang from a running start. He fell on his side, only to get up again. Dormach learned persistence and gained strength as he moved toward his final leap.

One day, Noreia was setting her laundry on a rock to dry when she looked up from her work. She was so surprised that she knocked over a bucket of water.

A gust of wind filled Dormach's bat-like wings. He soared over a great chasm where there were waterfalls and a forest of ancient ferns and palms. Then she could no longer see him in the distance. Dormach found his wings!

Another fine day, Dormach watched as Noreia was whittling a long branch to add to the roof. "Dormach, one day I will not be here to teach you!" Noreia said to the dragon who looked to her for guidance.

"Why not, Noreia?" asked the dragon. His wings drooped.

"Because...one day you will be a guardian and protector of the inhabitants of the Sea Realm," said Noreia. "Listen, Dormach. You must be motivated to lead for the right reasons, like defending your friends or preventing battles. You will one day be a great Dragon King, like your father, I am sure of it!"

The dragon nodded and went to his nest for a nap in the shade. He awoke to find his guardian sitting and tying a fishing spear. The sun had drained the princess' energy, and her smooth hands were worn with callouses.

"What are you thinking, Noreia?" asked Dormach.

"I am thinking about your progress with flying. Are you practicing your fire breathing, too?"

"Why do you ask?"

"The wind has picked up. Soon the dragons will be returning. We'll need your help with the campfire for this evening's roasted salmon," said Noreia.

By now, Dormach's flames and wind power were great enough to start a campfire from kindling. He stood over eight feet tall. Noreia had to tie down their dwelling, because Dormach's wings would produce a gust of wind.

When nine months had swept behind them, Dormach saw a strange ship from the north sailing toward the island. When he notified Noreia, she quickly gathered the mermaids and korrigana, the dragon elders, the dolphins, the cormorants, and the great blue herons of the bay.

Princess Noreia prepared a banquet to greet the ship's arrival. Coral goblets were fashioned for the feast by the fairies' men. Chowder made with fresh seaweed and kelp was to be served in abalone shells. Baskets of exotic mango and papaya were set out for her intended guests. Noreia dressed in a tattered gown that the mermaids had discovered in a sunken ship. The mermaids gave her pearls they had strung together with sailors' knots. Noreia still wore the gold necklace from her mother.

Noreia set a special place at the head of the table for her father. She told herself that she was being ridiculous, because he'd never said he would return. He merely promised to send supplies, not to arrive on the ship himself. That didn't stop her from hoping that he would. She was certain he loved her enough to want to see her again.

The low sun passed slowly over the fine banquet that she had prepared. The goblets cast deep purple shadows. The wind picked up, causing the great palms to sway. The tablecloth, made from a ship's sail, billowed and flapped. Fairies rushed to her side, arranging shells on the corners of the table and putting forks on the sailcloth linens.

Palms swayed from the pressure of the wind, and clouds covered the sun. Noreia hoped that her father's ship would survive the journey. His presence meant everything to her. She missed him. Noreia began a prayer to bring her father safely to her again.

Bless, first, the dragon to me dear,
And bless my father on the sea.
Praise the main sail that brought him near,
Take him to journey, here for me!

She sat down at the table, from which she thought she

could see the hull of her father's ship grow like a tiny toy in her outstretched hand. Alas, it was not a ship. It was merely a mirage. The ship's white sails were clouds. Its hull turned out to be a huge rock with a series of smaller ones in silhouette. The fog had deceived her. Noreia wept.

CHAPTER 27
The Flight Back

It had been ten months since Noreia had first helped the offspring of Draighean, the dragon queen. She still had not seen a ship approaching.

Dormach had grown from a small babe to an impressive dragon with a vast wingspan and a gentle demeanor. He had long before grown too tall for the nest near their shelter. He lay in front of Noreia's door each night.

On the last evening in March, the cold wind wrapped itself around the branches and rustled the ferns. The sky was a clear indigo behind the stars. When Dormach had finished gathering wood, a friend surprised Noreia at the campfire, sitting down upon a low lying boulder.

"General Westwyn," cried Noreia, "what brings you to our dwelling? Welcome to our gathering. And how do you fare, General Fogspell?"

"Good greetings and bad news, Your Highness! About Emerhill—" General Fogspell began.

"You have news of my father, and his kingdom?" asked Noreia. She looked out at the sea from which her father's ship had never appeared.

"Yes. I must tell you that the Kingdom of Emerhill will be the next kingdom under attack!"

"What do you mean?" Noreia asked, distraught.

"As general of the Dragon Guard, it is my business to know our enemies' plans," General Fogspell explained. "For a week, my scouts have dispatched messages from the Roc's conferences. There is a place where we listen, perching in the high redwoods close to the Silver Bridge. The Roc general, Nettlelurch, was speaking to his Roc lieutenant. I overheard their scheming while I was patrolling Fay Linn Island. He said they plan to attack the Kingdom of Emerhill in merely four weeks!"

"Why would the Rocs want to take over Emerhill?" asked Dormach.

"There is an old dragon saying, that whoever uses a spell from the Fairies' Spell Book can determine his own fate! The Roc King can rule over all the fairy kingdoms if no one stops him," Westwyn told them.

"From what I overheard, they want to rule your father's kingdom. Someone named Holocene—" said a dragon soldier.

"My father's in danger! Please, General, I implore you to help me save Emerhill! I need you to send some of your troops to help my family and kingdom," Noreia pleaded. "Our differences are great, General, but all of the fairy realms will be in jeopardy if the Rocs attack Emerhill.

"If the dragons help defend my father's kingdom," she continued, "I'm certain that my father will agree to help Dragonera in return. We must band together to defeat the Rocs' enormous military strength. We have no time to waste. We must gather our allies. In the name of dragonkind, you must help me!"

"Yes, we shall, in the name of fellowkind, Your Highness!" General Westwyn tipped his helmet in respect to her. "I shall send a carrier pigeon to the other side of the island, to warn Alvar and his troops. They, too, will need to prepare for the journey to Emerhill."

"And I shall send word to my soldiers and a message of warning to dragonkind!" said Fogspell before flying into the sky.

Noreia turned to look up at Dormach, who towered over her. His soft gaze comforted her.

"And Dormach is old enough now to join us in the Dragon Guard," the general added. There were cheers and applause from the elves and dragons. "Your friend Noreia was kind and wise to watch over you. When you were young, you might have been an easy target for King Roparz 's men," said Westwyn. "I'm sorry to bring up a terrible history, Noreia. However, your father did attempt to invade this island. He also killed Dormach's mother."

"Why did your father want to kill my mother?" asked Dormach.

"Because he was afraid. He was afraid of her, I think," said Noreia.

"Are you afraid of the Rocs, Noreia?" Dormach asked. His eyes revealed concern.

"Yes, I am afraid, but you must not fear. You must be strong, yes?" Noreia looked up to meet Dormach's eyes as she spoke. Dormach nodded. "My great grandparents built and ruled fairly in a castle called Lore, once located upon the shore of France where Emerhill Castle stands today. Now my father is in danger at Emerhill Castle. The Rocs are planning to attack Emerhill," Noreia repeated.

"What could happen to us?" asked Dormach.

"While you are here to protect me, I am safe. The Rocs know their strength is incapable of defeating you, Dormach. And you will not be alone. General Westwyn and General Alvar will lead their forces in a counterattack."

One of the dragon soldiers added a branch onto the embers of the fire.

"Are Rocs afraid of dragons?" Dormach asked, practicing a snarl. A trace of a smile on Noreia blinked and was gone.

"Yes, that is their weakness, Dormach. They should be afraid."

"Why do they fear me?" asked the young dragon with a serious expression.

"Because you are ferocious!" Noreia told him, smiling.

"Let me help you, Noreia. You have been my mother," Dormach said. "My wings are strong and my endurance good. In a few days, I can reach this Castle Emerhill and help you save your father. I remember well the stories you have told me. I want to meet your family, across the ocean." Dormach gazed into at the campfire and then turned back to Noreia.

"You are wise *and* strong. Then, yes, you may take me as far as Emerhill's castle gates, where you and I can rescue my father. You are old enough to defend us now. No harm will come to you there, my dear friend," said Noreia.

"I will fly you to the castle, Noreia," said the dragon again, arching his wings. He was magnificent in the firelight.

The sky was speckled with bright stars. "And you will not

have to do it alone, Dormach. We will be beside you as you fly!" said Baldwyr, the dragon scout.

"We will fly in formation behind you, as swift as arrows!" added Fogspell, now perched on a nearby branch. The moon played its light through the branches. The wind was strong. Such a current would be needed for Dormach's wings to take them there.

"Wait! If you fly in such a formation, my father's guards will spot you before we even reach the castle gate. However, if we hide the troops on the island of Doire, we may still have a chance," said Noreia. "The isle is northwest of Emerhill Bay. Dormach and I shall fly ahead. There I will learn my father's true mind. If he accepts me and the magic being I have helped, I will send word to your army via Pierre, my carrier seagull."

"Excellent idea, Princess. When we receive your message, we can advance and hide in Emerhill forest!"

"What about weapons?" asked Sergeant Nilda, adjusting a quiver of arrows around her shoulder.

"What will we need? I know there are two main towers that face the Atlantic, well guarded by the king's best archers. We can support their army by guarding the northeast tower. It is surrounded by Father's forest."

"Where can we get enough arrows to fight the Rocs?" asked Antoine, an elfin dragon rider.

"Such a good question. I will bring along one of my finest fletchers," said Sergeant Nilda.

"I'm sorry we can't fly with you, Noreia. But, we will fight alongside you before long," said Alvar.

"Yes, General. Be wise and careful. Beware that it is March in Emerhill Kingdom. Brittany is known for the force and power of its winds. The sea current alone can sink a ship! When you arrive in Brittany, you can fill your water flasks by the brook that runs over the farmlands. Fare you well!" said Noreia.

She stood on a precipice near the roots of the banyan tree where they had made a home. It overlooked the ravine where Dormach had claimed the sky for the first time. She hoisted herself from a rock onto Dormach's enormous back. Once the two had risen into the sky, the fairies and elves scrambled to the hills to wave goodbye.

Dormach's wide wings cast a shadow over the ridged landscape. His great shadow rippled and expanded over cliffs and valleys. Chasms and cliffs slipped away, as the frantic ocean stirred beneath them. Dormach's wings swooped through the clouds and into the sky. Noreia saw her dreams realized in that instant. Dormach would lead her to victory one day.

Noreia watched the gathered Dragon Guard depart from the forested side of the island. Fogspell led the dragon clan in a triangular formation, his helmet sparkling. His friends fell in behind him. They left the rocks, cliffs, and sand. They left the trees, swooping into the air like giant bats, glowing in the light of the moon.

CHAPTER 28

Her Father's Kingdom

Noreia and Dormach sailed through the night sky over many islands. Below Dormach's leathery wings, they followed merchant ships in order to stay on course. They hugged the crags and bays of the coastline and headed northwest of the Spanish coast. As they rounded a corner, a familiar bay appeared, and the little island of Lismoire appeared, half hidden under its canopy of trees. Princess Noreia saw tiny rivers emptying into the Atlantic Sea and seagulls winging over the waves.

Memories flooded her mind as she flew toward her family. She had been gone a year! Noreia was amazed at how small Emerhill Kingdom was, now that she was older and more knowledgeable about the world. She recalled the long hours she had spent with her brother Argantael, playing along the beach. She could see Stalwart's water cave, and the place they had met. How he had laughed and roared when he saw her!

She had a strange longing she did not want to feel again. How could she face her father, and what would he say?

Marcelina's cottage, the rocky beach, the village, and her father's forest came into view. Noreia saw a flat plain ahead and touched Dormach's left wing to direct him. Dormach responded to her gesture, sweeping over tiny fences and a rambling stone wall. A farmer's neat furrows made patterns on the ground.

Aiming for an open field, Dormach had trouble slowing his speed. Gliding over the frosted treetops, Noreia clung to his neck. They skimmed the trees as Noreia dodged the branches. Dormach slowed enough to let her slip off onto a grassy bluff surrounded by trees. Then he circled around to where she had leapt off. The tall grass was wild and dry, and the distant castle was high above them. Dormach landed gently near there. Noreia gathered berries and other fruits while Dormach fished or gathered large branches for the campfire.

"We must part now, my friend! We shall meet again, when my father has changed his mind. I will send word to you when it is safe for you to fly to the castle."

"Very well, Noreia. You have given me my life, and I am grateful. I will return for you!" said Dormach. He softly bent his neck to her. Noreia kissed his nose, and waved goodbye.

His great wings drifted over the field toward the trees until he disappeared. He would hide among the rocky caves and cliffs of the seashore. Dormach would recognize them, Noreia knew, because she had described them well. She smiled proudly and blew him a kiss.

Emerhill Castle was farther away than it had seemed from the air, but the princess was no stranger to climbing cliffs. As Dormach circled away, Noreia began the long hike up the trail to her home.

The guards nodded their acknowledgment of her. The archers on the gatehouse scurried over the battlements to secure a view of her. There were shouts as the laborers came running to peer through the great iron gates. Although they knew about her father's strictness and anger, they had known her kindness, too.

A group of knights rode out to escort her through the gates of the royal castle, followed by a team of guards carrying shields of hand wrought brass. On the path to the inner bailey and main castle, brightly dressed soldiers carried trumpets whose

Fanfare soon would announce her arrival. Noreia felt grateful to these men, who acknowledged the princess they had known so long ago. She had to convince herself she belonged there.

In the main hall, the butler came forward. "Why, this is our own Noreia, the princess who long ago disappeared from our shores!" A maid from the dining hall pulled Duana from the kitchen.

"Absurd! You can't convince me with your stories this time!" Duana adjusted her spectacles with hands covered in flour. "The little girl I knew couldn't really be here, could she?"

"I am glad to be back again, Duana!" said Noreia. Duana was too astonished to speak, throwing her arms around the young woman for a tearful embrace.

As they chatted in the main hall, Argantael ran in. "Noreia! I thought I would never see you alive again, my lost sister," he cried. Then he ran out again, and brought his mother from the music room. "Mother, there's someone I need you to meet," he said, escorting her into the hall.

"I can't take another imposter, Argantael! I can't bear it!" said the queen.

"This is your daughter, Mother. Noreia has returned from the island."

She stood back a pace, stunned. "I was afraid you would never return to us, my daughter!" said Queen Ceana, cradling her daughter's face in her hands. Tears filled her eyes.

"Mother, I'm here. I've returned from the island. I'm safe now," Noreia said, embracing her mother.

"My child! Why did you leave me? No one has looked after you at all. Are you hungry? Where have you been? Let me look at you. Dimitri, do send for some water, *tout de suite*!"

"Yes, Your Highness! Immediately." And the butler was off.

"Argantael, I must speak to Father," Noreia told him.

"I hope it isn't about dragons again," he replied.

She stepped away from him. "Yes, I have a dragon friend. He is the child of a dragon mother who was slain on the island!"

Then the princess noticed her white haired grandmother, stooped over a cane, walking slowly toward them.

"I don't understand," said the elderly queen. "Are you a ghost?"

"No, Grandmother Gwenaelle. I'm really here. It's Noreia, your granddaughter."

"Wasn't she lost years ago, Argantael? She was killed by a terrible dragon!"

"The dragons are my friends, grandmother, and they could be our allies, too," said Noreia. "Oh, how I've missed you." Noreia hugged her grandmother and held her hand. "We are together once again," she said, but the white haired queen mother just looked confused, and went out to her garden.

"Do not worry about Grandmother. It was so hard for her, your leaving. She has kept worrying and wondering when you would return," said Argantael.

"Does she really think I died?" Noreia asked.

"She is getting older, Noreia," said her brother. "There'll be times when she'll be more aware of you."

"I miss her more now than I did on that island!" exclaimed Noreia.

"Is it true what you just said? The dragons are good beings who could be our allies?" Argantael asked.

"Yes, Argantael. They are good beings, the same as you or I. They have learned to fear humans," said the princess.

"Noreia, I don't understand how you survived."

"I raised the dragonling on the island called Dragonera. He is full grown now. I lived in the forest armed by the books we read together."

"You are the most courageous person I know, Noreia," said Argantael, embracing her. "How long have you been gone?"

"I think it's been a year, Argantael."

Her brother Dalwyn entered the hall and bowed before her. "We meet again! Noreia, I am so glad you have returned. While you were away, I traveled to the north of Emerhill."

"And what did you find?"

"I traveled to the Sea of Iroise, where they tell stories of great men," Dalwyn told her. "I found an ancient archipelago. I found the Bay of Lismoire, a crowded sardine port. And stories of the land of Bohemia! I have brought tapestries for the walls and a new falcon for Father. For you, I have a bolt of Irish linen I traded for in Normandy. I knew you would return!"

"Thank you! How kind. You are an explorer now, Dalwyn. How did you know I would ever return?" Noreia asked.

"I hoped....I just wished that you would come back," Dalwyn struggled to say. "I was scared for you, Noreia."

They heard the sound of footsteps approaching. The guards, in green doublets and golden, feathered hats, entered in lockstep. Each of them turned as if upon a coin, forming a row that framed the hallway.

Then they escorted her through the main hall to the throne room and her father. When they entered the room, Noreia hesitated. A long white beard covered his neck, and a green circular cape was fastened at his shoulders. He held a scepter with a silver dragon overlaid around its hilt, where a helmeted wild hawk perched. Courtiers stood in groups around the room. By the time she arrived at the main gate of the castle, Noreia had not seen her father for eleven months and three weeks.

"Noreia, you have returned!" There was an awkward silence.

"I am glad to see you again," Noreia said.

"It has been, for your mother and me, a difficult year! And you, my dear, were welcome here all the while," said King Roparz from his throne.

"Why did you not send a ship for me? I waited for a messenger with supplies. I waited to honor you with a feast," Noreia said.

"Eleven months we searched for you. I sent my best captains, but they never found the island, because none could navigate the course to you. They have been sent to the dungeon. You are my dear daughter, who is my greatest treasure. Welcome home, Noreia!"

Her father signaled for his page to bring a tray of food for her, a fine array of fruits, French bread, and pastries.

"Let me look at you," he said. King Roparz turned to his wife. "My daughter has returned to me, Ceana! You have grown up, Noreia. Hasn't she?"

"Roparz, she is too slender, and her dress is torn," said her mother.

"Father, yes, I'm here!" said Noreia. "Right here, prepared to be your daughter again. I'm glad to be home, but now I need to tell you something important!" Her eyes stayed fixed on her father's.

"Roparz, this is our beloved daughter, and we must listen to her!" said the queen. She sat in silence upon her throne, awaiting what Noreia would say.

"The Rocs are going to attack Emerhill! The Dragon Guard, General Alvar, and his army of elfin warriors will help you. We—"

"What? You must have left those horrible dragons behind you! You must have wakened to your senses!" the king said, taking a bite of a golden apple.

"No, I have brought the dragon. He is grown, and the dragons are my friends and companions. They are your allies!" the princess said.

The king threw the apple down the marble steps. It rolled and stopped at her feet.

"Such impertinence! Where is this beast?"

"Somewhere safe!" Noreia said. "The dragons have

agreed to provide their assistance in battling the enemy. You must trust me that—"

"Trust *you*! You befriended a vicious, conniving beast. You allowed a dragon to kill a hundred sailors. A disaster at sea occurred in our kingdom because of your carelessness! Help, indeed!" King Roparz strode over the smooth marble platform and down the steps to his daughter.

"Roparz! Noreia is our daughter," the queen exclaimed. "That she cares for the sea creatures is understandable. She found a helpless dragonling and wanted only to save its life. Surely you can understand that?"

"Daughter, think," Roparz said more gently. "Think of how you could live here in comfort with those who care for you. Tell me where to find the dragon. Do not run away from me again, please. Abandon the creature and stay at home." The king studied his daughter's face. Then he touched her shoulder.

"It was useless for me to bring you my help. You have not changed! You are still impossible to understand!" Noreia shouted, pulling herself away from him.

"Noreia! Your father only meant—"

"Mother, he doesn't care. He'll always blame the dragons for that storm! He won't admit he was wrong, even now," said the princess.

"Don't speak to your mother that way," the king said.

"Father!" Dalwyn said. "I must bring to light a fact of which you are not aware. When you and I were on the island of Fay Linn—"

"Enough, Dalwyn," the king interrupted. "You leave me no choice, Noreia. You shall be jailed upon these shores, in the southeast guard tower, to prevent you from returning to that island. Now my villagers will be safe again."

"No, Father!" shouted Dalwyn. "How could you?" By now, many courtiers had assembled in the throne room, gesturing and arguing about the princess. He fought his way through the crowd. "Leave her alone!" he shouted to the guards. He placed himself between the guards and his startled sister. "Leave her alone!"

"The princess of Emerhill!" said a foppish lord. "Surely he's not going to jail his own daughter!"

"The king could change his mind!" a graceful lady exclaimed. Noreia seized the moment, yanking her shoulders away from the guard holding her. She faced the throne.

"Admit you were wrong! I knew that Stalwart was innocent, because I was listening to the Royal Council. I heard you give in to the crowd. They wanted to blame the dragon to avenge the sailors who died on your ship. It was the storm, Father!"

"I don't have to listen to this nonsense!" The king looked away.

"Yes, you will! I know the ship was in disrepair on the night of the Great Storm! I remember the carpenter's testimony. Its very floorboards were rotting. Stalwart was only diving for food that night, not destroying ships!"

"Noreia! Noreia!" Argantael shouted, placing himself

between the advancing guards and his frightened sister. "Father, you cannot do this! You can't throw your own daughter in a locked room!"

"Argantael, you are trying my patience!" said King Roparz.

"You embarrass me, Father!" shouted Dalwyn. The crowd was silent and still. Then it parted for the elderly queen mother.

Queen Gwenaelle addressed her son. "Roparz! You will set this girl free. She has done nothing to offend the kingdom. It is merely your own pride!"

"That's enough! Take her to the southeast tower!"

"There's going to be a war, Father," cried Noreia. "Our kingdom is in danger!" Her hands shackled, the princess stood before him, tears welling in her eyes.

"Noreia, you may never return to Dragonera!" said the king.

"What a hypocrite you are, Roparz!" the queen said. She stood and walked down the marble steps from the platform, placing her hands upon her daughter's face and wiping away her tears. The courtiers shouted in protest, but the king was silent then, watching his daughter being led away to the tower.

The stoic king watched as his wife led her ladies in waiting across the floor toward the archway. Her ladies-in-waiting wept as Noreia passed by them.

CHAPTER 29

A Captive

Armed with spears, the guards led the princess down a long corridor and then up a flight of stairs. When they passed the archway leading to her room, Noreia turned her head to look back. Longing pulled at her, but she did not cry. She knew from the solemn way the soldiers marched that she was headed for a dim stairwell and up to the tower room. Her eyes flashed to the left and right. She memorized the turns of the cold stairway. Glowing torches led the guards through the darkness.

When the guards opened an iron grating, the hinges made a high pitched noise. Then Noreia heard the slam of the gate behind her. The guards left her cold and alone. She was too tired to fight anyone. She sat down on a wooden bench against the wall and she did not weep.

When she awoke, moonlight cast shadows through the barred windows. A draft chilled her shoulders, and she blew on her hands to stay warm. She looked around, noticing that the room had been cleared of any ropes or other tools she might use to escape. Was all hope truly lost?

She looked up to a lancet window from which a strand of light fell onto the walls, cascading over the rough floorboards. A dragonfly flew from the window to the princess's outstretched hand and settled on her palm.

The dragonfly playfully led the young princess. It was like a hopeful guide to her failing spirits. Noreia laughed as the dragonfly fluttered by a hanging lantern. She lit the candle and followed the creature through the shadows, along the tower's curving walls to a small wooden door. Through the bars of the window, she noticed that the door led to the battlements. With her ear pressed against it, she could overhear the gossip of the guards.

"I can't keep my eyes open. Hear any news about the princess?" muttered the first guard.

"Do you mean the one we thought had drowned at sea?" said the second guard.

"Yes, of course. She and the king had an argument. I heard they put her in this tower. I am uncertain for how long!" said a third guard.

"How terrible!" said the second one. "She's just a child."

"The king seems inconsolable now. He should sleep, but he is just staring out at the sea!" said the first guard.

"Might the king change his mind?" asked the second guard.

"I don't know. If you hear anything more, let me know," said the third.

There was a loud march of feet then, as the guards made their rounds along the battlements between the towers. Once they had walked away, Noreia could not wait another minute. She held her breath and pressed her weight against the door. Her pulse pounded as she heard the door creak, but it did not open.

The princess spun around, searching, fearing her luck was gone. At least the guards had left her with the helmet, a quiver of arrows, and her sword. She thrust her cold hands into the pockets of her cape to keep them warm. When she found the beautiful green pearl the fairy in the woods had given her, Noreia clasped the pearl to her chest, a silent celebration of the great hope in her heart.

Noreia took a deep breath. Remembering the way the fairy had told her to use the green pearl, she said a quiet prayer and rolled it to the other side of the door.

Then something extraordinary happened. The flickering dragonfly slipped through the door's barred window. A bright green light shone through the keyhole. Then the doorknob turned. The door creaked, opening slowly. The cold night air touched her face. Noreia saw nothing at first through the fog. Then a warm glow of green light reminded her of the presence of magic.

The splendid Fairy Rayenna stood before her again. A beacon of light, the fairy emitted radiance as her soft gray wings fluttered gracefully. She took Noreia's hand and led her out of the small tower room onto the steps to a high turret. They ascended to the roof, overlooking her father's holdings. She looked back to the tower citadels that held the flag and the stone turrets perched upon the defensive walls of the castle. The guards were standing watch.

Noreia gasped as the shining green dragonfly reappeared

once more, landing calmly in Fairy Rayenna 's hand. The grand fairy petted his back with her finger. She whispered to her little messenger, who hovered and buzzed before flying out of sight.

"Noreia, I can help you. You'll need this pouch of changing dust. It's a special kind of magic powder that, when sprinkled upon a living being, transforms that creature. It must be kept safe." The fairy's long robes billowed in the cold wind.

"Do you trust me with such powerful magic?" asked the girl, rubbing her arms for warmth.

"Of course. Remember who you are, Noreia! You will know in your heart when the time comes. The spell is kept safe as well, in an old volume no one has disturbed for a hundred years. I trust you," she repeated. As she spoke, Rayenna 's sparkling, cloudy image was vanishing.

"Wait, please!" cried Noreia. "What do you mean? I don't know how to cast any... spells!" Noreia unconsciously felt for the small book in her purse. There was all the magic she would need. As the liquid image of the fairy disappeared, Noreia noticed the dragonfly beckoning her to the roof of the watchtower. From there, the fortress walls had views of all the stone walls and terraces. Archers atop the main gate had propped themselves up to stay alert.

Morning fog moved in around the other watchtowers, weaving into the forest. Noreia remembered the way the dragonfly had hovered so gracefully over Fairy Rayenna 's palm. It had settled there so calmly, without fear.

"Of course," thought the princess, smiling. "She sent that dragonfly to find him!" She could hardly believe her eyes. Winging toward her was the dragon, his amber eyes flashing. His gentle face was kind and familiar indeed. She tore the ribbon from her hair, using it as a bright green flag to show him where she was standing.

"Dormach," she whispered into the wind. "You are here for me!"

CHAPTER 30

𝔄 𝔇istant 𝔖hore

"Stop!" bellowed the eldest guard. "Men, hold your fire! That is the king's daughter you are shooting at!"

The dragon soared onto the tower, his eyes glowing. He beat his vast wings to swoop to her as he landed on the defensive wall. He waited for her to climb onto his back with her helmet and sword. He was a majestic creature, his amber wings illuminated by the moon.

The guards scrambled over the walls of the castle, some pointing up at the winged being, now airborne. Some of the astonished archers aimed their arrows at Dormach, sending their sharp flints through the air with the swift force of the wind. Noreia stole a glance back at her father's castle, the place of her birth. She saw the strange sight of her home, a lonely fortress swimming in the fog. How strange and remote it seemed from the world of struggle behind her and the battle that would soon occur.

Hovering upon the north wind, the pair flew above the night watchmen at the gate. Beyond the handlaid walls of the outer courtyard, they dove over the green cliffs of Emerhill and glided among the clouds.

Flying over great ships' masts, they headed north of the kingdom, toward the island of Doire. The princess and

Dormach stayed silent for the sunrise.

Dormach hovered, looking out upon the waves. Tiny white ships rode the sea as they followed the coastline to stay on course. The soft light of the sunrise was calming to her. The gentle breeze caused by the dragon's wings made her drowsy. Noreia's shoulders drooped, yet she forced herself to stay alert.

She sensed that Dormach's wings were weary. She said, as they followed the cliffs, high above the ocean, "Are you tired of flying, Dormach? Even dragons get tired, I know. I can't keep my eyes open. We can land upon a field near here, and safely hide from the Rocs."

They flew inland, over half timbered houses nestled in the trees that dotted the countryside.

"Let us stay here to sleep until tomorrow," Dormach said.

"Yes, I'm afraid our journey will have to wait 'til sunrise tomorrow," Noreia said, yawning. The dragon landed on a field near the sardine port of Duarnenez, where her father used to fish.

"In the morning, we can fly to Doire Island, where our allies are waiting," said Dormach.

"I'm sorry I couldn't convince Father," she whispered.

"You tried your best on my behalf, Noreia. Thank you!"

She examined her surroundings. Upon the soft grass of a farmer's field, she heard distant sounds of cowbells, chickens, and sheep. She was soon fast asleep, under Dormach's wing.

CHAPTER 32
𝔐agical 𝔄llies

"Princess Noreia?" A soldier standing over her shook her awake. She leapt for her sword and faced him, but instantly recognized the long red beard and hammered breastplate of General Alvar.

"It is day!" shouted the general. "We must fly away quickly to reach your father's palace, before the Rocs attack! Here, Noreia, take this bronze helmet and shield."

"They are both well wrought. Whose helmet is this?" Noreia asked.

"It was my father's helmet," Dormach told her. "He would have wanted you to make good use of it. The shield was in General Fogspell's family for two centuries."

"Thank you, Dormach! You honor me. They will bring us victory!" Noreia proclaimed.

"What's happened? Are they here?" said Noreia, rubbing her eyes. She looked around her at the company of Dragonera troops.

"We saw the Rocs flying over Doire Isle and waited for your message," General Westwyn explained. "Fairy Rayenna sent her dragonfly with a message, saying you were a captive."

"We knew we needed to advance," added Alvar. "We knew you would not be far from your father's castle. We were fortunate to find you here."

"I just don't know what I should do. I respect my father, but how can I help him if he dismisses me in such a way?" Noreia pondered. "But...he is my father."

"What can we do? Is it too late?" asked Dormach.

"I fear they have already captured the castle!" said Alvar. "We need to attack from the air!"

"How did I let this happen?" cried Noreia, throwing on her cape and helmet. She paused to sit down on a stone wall. "My family and kingdom are worth fighting for! I must defend Emerhill. It needs me."

"That's not all Rayenna's note said," said Westwyn. "General Fogspell's guard is advancing to our shores to help us! They wait for us to join with the elves' dragon riders. They await your return at your father's hunting grounds."

"Once my elfin archers take out the Rocs guarding the towers, our foot soldiers can attack!" said Alvar.

"May your archers' arrows be swift and sure!" said Noreia. "Tell me your plan, General Alvar! How do you propose we get in to help the Emerhill guards? Shall we fly in with our dragons?"

"No, not yet. We can use ladders to scale the walls," said Sergeant Nilda.

"Where can we get ladders?" asked Noreia, pondering.

"You forget, Your Highness, that we elves are master builders, with a specialty in tree houses!" Alvar said. The general unfurled his map of the castle. "Once we reach the tower here, Sergeant Nilda 's soldiers will scale the walls up to the battlements. Her soldiers will surprise the Rocs guarding each tower," he explained.

"Brilliant idea, General! We'll overwhelm them in numbers," said Noreia.

"There are Roc guards posted at each tower," repeated Alvar. "Once the soldiers take out the remaining guards, my dragon riders can fight our way down to the central castle courtyard!" The elf soldiers cheered his statement as they gathered around a small group of trees.

Noreia was silent. She nodded thoughtfully.

"But there must be hundreds of Rocs guarding the castle!" she said, pulling her cape over her shoulders. She frowned, looking over the hills at the soft image of the castle in the fog.

"That's when we send in our airmen, riding upon the dragons. The dragons will come to us at the castle courtyard, for a surprise attack!" said Dormach.

Noreia helped the general roll up the map. "Do not worry about the enemy seeing the dragons, Your Highness!" said Westwyn. "The dragons will fly to the north side of Emerhill Bay, where they will hide beneath the water's surface. Our airmen will hide in the caves. When they spot Rayenna 's dragonfly, the men riding dragons will make their attack!"

"Then we must go, now, to save Emerhill!" cried Noreia. "We shall drive away those who threaten my father's kingdom. Then dragonkind, humankind, and our friends the elves of the forest shall fight as one!"

"We shall, as one force, rescue King Roparz and free

Emerhill!" Baldwyr exclaimed.

With a running start, the elfin riders leaped upon the backs of the winged dragons. In the warmth of the early sunlight, the dragons' huge webbed wings fanned out as they followed in formation. They formed a triangle in the sky and flew toward the caves.

Noreia stepped up onto Dormach's back. The dragon's head lifted as they took off into the bright open sky, heading for the forest. Dormach's scales gleamed with the sun's golden touch.

By the time they were approaching the valley beside the forest, the sun was higher in the sky, hidden in the clouds. The day was crisp, and the cold air wakened Noreia.

She was ready.

CHAPTER 33
The Great Battle

Soaring through the air, Noreia realized Dormach couldn't fly over the castle without alerting the guards. As they approached the castle, she took out the blue gray pearl Grandmother Marcelina had given her. She said a prayer to Xiang, the unseen dragon named for his power to rule the fog:

> *Father's loss will raise our swords,*
> *And armies lead the days,*
> *Xiang, Majesty of fog,*
> *Cloak us with your cloudy haze!*

Noreia saw a silver gleam slip through the clouds. For a moment, Xiang had emerged like a ray of sun in the sky. Fog enveloped them, shielding the two friends from the guards.

Noreia noticed that none of the Emerhill guards were in place at the towers. Perched on the high walls, Rocs sat like vultures, grouped in clusters upon the towers, eyeing all who approached. Countless more Rocs sat in the gangly trees surrounding the castle gate. Noreia shivered, aware of the cruelty in their eyes.

She thought of the night of the storm, when the Rocs had attacked. Even her father had been helpless against them. A surge of fear rushed through her when she thought of her family in danger. What would her father do to escape them? How could she save her mother, grandmother, and brothers?

They reached the king's forest, where they heard songbirds circling the trees. Below the northwestern tower, they landed and found the elves' camp, hidden by mighty oaks.

"We'll need to send as many soldiers as we can up to battle the Roc guards, General Alvar!" said Noreia. She slipped the quiver strap over her shoulder and picked up her bow. "There are hundreds more Rocs here. I'll need a multitude of soldiers!"

"I'll send in more of my archers to take out some of their troops!" said Alvar, putting on his helmet.

Noreia nodded to Alvar and followed as he led his soldiers through the cover of the foliage to the foot of the northwestern tower. Leaves crunched as the Roc guards positioned themselves, patrolling the towers above them. Tree branches moved in the whispering wind.

A strange stillness surrounded them. Noreia felt the throbbing of her heart as she tried to concentrate on her footing and her breath. On Alvar 's command, the archers fired. Flurries of arrows arced over the walls to meet their targets. In answer, Rocs screeched and flapped their wings, scattering from the towers. Some fell to the ground.

The elf archers, who were hiding in the forest, were struck by dirt and rocks as the Rocs flew over them. The elf foot soldiers put their ladders in place and crept up the wall to the battlements. Some of the Rocs were still in their places on the tower roofs. The Rocs counterattacked, fending the elves off with swords. Wounded elves tumbled from the battlements to the forest floor.

Noreia surveyed the battlefield. The Rocs had fought fiercely from the beginning, and hundreds of feathered soldiers' bodies littered the courtyard. The blood of the elfin troops ran between the stones in rivers. A wound of grief was in her heart. She needed to honor them with a victory.

Noreia looked up, as the wind howled in the trees. She feared the worst. Dark purple shadows moved over the canopy of trees. Something was on its way. There was a moment of darkness as the Rocs, panicked, and flew away. Terrible cries came from their fallen soldiers.

Out of a cloudless sky came a glorious sight: a glimpse of bronze helmets, elegant wings, and flowing capes flying over the trees. Dragons and their riders were flying valiantly onto the battlements, or perching on the tower roofs. General Alvar was astride a dragon named Raijin, and Sargent Nilda rode on the back of one called Enlil. Raijin's blue scales flashed as he soared over the trees. Enlil's golden wings propelled him, as the sunlight illuminated them. More elves flew in, their green capes swirling. They flew in a pack of tremendous winged creatures. Never had Noreia seen such splendid wings!

General Westwyn landed and gathered his troops in the castle courtyard, ready to join the battle. "Alvar, I need you to continue the battle with the Roc guards, keeping them from regaining control of the towers."

"Yes, General," said Alvar.

"Look for their leader, General Nettlelurch," warned Noreia. "I'll take out their guards in the lower courtyard and will make my way to the throne room. I pray that my father is still alive!"

Noreia led Dormach into the sky, gathering momentum to strike the Roc guards. Riding their dragons over the castle, Alvar, Nilda, and Noreia swept through the clouds, the wind at their heels. Nettlelurch, too, took off into the air with his cronies. His armored flock rose into the fog, but Noreia was ready. Her sword was swift and sure. She wielded it as she rode astride Dormach. Noreia fought off the hostile birds with skill and finesse.

The Rocs were clever soldiers who fought fiercely to maintain their claim of the inner court. Nilda soared in astride Enlil. He gritted his teeth as he sustained scrapes from the Rocs' daggers and claws. Helmeted Rocs struck the dragons right and left with their beaks and huge talons. The dragons reared back, stomping their feet upon the pavers. They flew in repeatedly to strike their enemies. The seabirds retreated as Sargent Nilda pressed her soldiers toward the western side of the castle. Both elf and Roc soldiers fell to their deaths.

Valiant elves flung their long swords at the last remaining Roc guards, who fell dead upon the courtyard, far below the castle walls.

"Watch out! "Alvar yelled to Noreia as a band of Rocs emerged from behind the columns, bursting out into the courtyard, brandishing their swords. Up they flew, hovering over the battle below them.

Noreia's instincts were tuned from her life on Dragonera. Her strong arms fought against the last remaining birds, huge and menacing as they were. As her sword sped through the air, feathers went flying, falling to the pavers of the courtyard.

As the dragons advanced, the last three Rocs fought fiercely, defending the fortress they had taken. They backed away, closer and closer to the throne room door, by the columned walkway. As Noreia dove forward to fight with every ounce of strength she had, she raised her sword as high and as swiftly as she could.

Westwyn stabbed the first of the three Rocs in a flurry of feathers. A feathered carcass slumped to the ground. Noreia recoiled from the many dead she recognized, their blood dripping upon the cobblestones. Then came her shining sword, thrusting left and right, defending herself astride Dormach. Arrows flew past his torso. He was wounded by the point of a blade.

Some of the birds faded away in clouds of sparkling black dust that dissolved into thin air. There was an eerie silence. Noreia heard the rustle of the leaves and the howl of the cold wind. She surveyed the battlefield, seeing the huge bodies of lifeless dragons. There were dead Emerhill soldiers still gripping their swords, and piles of weapons, dull and stained with blood.

Yet Noreia sensed there was more danger lurking. She stepped across the stone courtyard, covered with fallen

Emerhill guards and elfin soldiers and the carcasses of defeated Rocs. She crept toward the outside stairs to the throne room door. Down she stepped, from stair to stair.

At the foot of the stairs lay a lifeless General Alvar. How horrible can a battle be when one so wise and good, who has stood against evil, receives such a fate? There was blood around him and on his clothes. Noreia held the red haired warrior in her arms and then, sensing danger, set him gently down.

Anger grew in her heart. Her head felt feverish and her pulse beat in her chest. Her fury rose from within.

She heard the leaves in the trees. There, across from her before the columned walkway, was the one Roc she had most feared.

Noreia saw him before her, fierce as ever. Nettlelurch was prepared for battle, in his iron helmet. He held a dagger in his sharp claw.

"We meet again, Princess!" Nettlelurch taunted. "Put up your sword!"

Noreia raised her weapon. "You will never take my father's throne, you vulture!"

"Well, now. Look who's calling people names," the bird answered. "*En guard!*" Nettlelurch was a scraggly bird, but he puffed his chest proudly.

"Let's see what you're made of, General!" Noreia shouted. "This time, only swords. No claws or beaks may be used in this duel!"

"R-r-r!" he snarled at her. "Have it your way, Noreia. It

can be a fair fight, then. But remember, you must accept defeat. If you lose, the Kingdom of Emerhill will be my master's claim."

"And General, you will accept *my* condition. If you lose, you and your army of ruffians must stay away from every Fairy Realm. You shall return to the small isle of birds from where you came!"

"Very well, then! You shall have your duel," Nettlelurch said.

"My friend Dormach will be our witness, and Nilda my second." Noreia nodded, taking in a deep breath. The two fighters placed themselves in a ready stance.

"*En guard!*" yelled Nilda. The elves stood on the high towers and battlements. Noreia heard the swoosh of the dragons' heavy green wings coming closer through the sky to witness the duel. She saw the glowing eyes of her elfin friends watching from the trees.

"*Allez!*" Darter, one of the Roc general's minions, announced, and Nettlelurch advanced instantly. Noreia's blade parried the attack. She leapt onto a stairway, fighting off his broadsword in a series of parries. Then Noreia's shining sword pierced Nettlelurch 's shoulder, missing the tip of his wing as he dodged her. He dropped his dagger. He struggled, flapping his wings to avoid her. With one last effort, he grabbed his dagger from the ground where it had fallen.

"I'm wounded!" snapped Nettlelurch as Noreia claimed her footing. He staggered back, unable to fly.

Noreia was glad she had won and that Nettlelurch was finished. She turned and walked away from the place where he lay.

"Is that the best you can do, Princess?" said a deep, throaty voice. "Not much, considering that the King of Emerhill's well being is at stake." Nettlelurch broke into a cackle.

In a flash, Noreia's sword was upright, striking through the air. Holocene's one good claw and his broadsword slashed wildly as he lunged forward, again and again. His strength stood against hers, her heart against his cunning. He was stronger, his rusted broadsword pressing hard against her long sword.

Swoosh! Noreia's sword shone as it sliced through the air, bright as the sun. Dormach watched as she spun and lunged, swiping at the Roc general. Nettlelurch countered her moves, his wounded wing tucked against his chest. However, his grip weakened as he defended himself against her thrusts. Noreia's father's throne would not fall to the claws of such a villain.

Noreia's intention was strong and her sword was sure. And Nettlelurch was badly wounded. He cowered from her, staggering off to a corner of the courtyard. His feathers around his left claw were bloodied.

"Go on, Princess. Go to your father again!" shouted Nettlelurch as she walked away. "I warn you that you're still too late. My master is on the throne now!"

"Stay here, Dormach, please," said Noreia. "We may need to make a hurried escape."

"Yes, Princess. You have done well," he said. Dormach flew up, perching himself at the top of a citadel.

Princess Noreia sped through the empty corridor and into the door to the Main Hall. The Rocs' crest hung from the roof beams, and the chairs were strewn with gray feathers. She did not dare to utter a syllable. She turned a corner into the throne room and gasped.

CHAPTER 36

The Roc King

Holocene, the Roc King, was perched on the back of the king's throne, now covered in claw marks. He was draped in her father's cape. Shredded curtains blocked out patches of sunlight, which fell in streaks over the thrones. Iron candleholders lay overturned. Emerhill's banners, once proudly displayed, had been yanked away and torn into rags. A Gothic window was left open to the chilling wind.

The room was filled with guards and attendants in shackles. Courtiers, jesters, musicians, and servants alike wore chains as the Roc guards led them toward the dungeon. Even her father's soldiers marched in chains.

"Let me look at you!" Holocene said.

"What have you done with my father?" the princess demanded, stepping forward. "And where are my brothers? My mother? Answer me!"

"I'd like to think of this as an opportunity, wouldn't you?" asked the bird ironically, glaring at her. As she came closer to the candlelight, Noreia saw the Rocs gathered behind him. Several of them stood atop a large table, counting gold coins, pearls, and finery stolen from the king's courtiers.

"How in the world? What do you mean?" asked Noreia. A glowing series of eyes appeared out of the shadows behind the throne where King Roparz once sat. The Rocs stood by, throwing large shadows upon the walls.

"Easy. A simple trade! Something for me for something you want back," said the menacing hawk. His cronies cackled slyly, their feathers rough and scraggly. Holocene's eyes glowered. Noreia's mind spun.

"What have you done to him? If you've harmed him in any way, I'll—"

"You'll what? Kill me? Go away without your father, King of Emerhill? No, you'll do just as I want. I will rule over the sea creatures along with the other fairy kingdoms. *I* will control Dragonera, Fay Linn, and Lismoire," said the terrible seabird. "Am I forgetting one? I guess I almost forgot Emerhill, tiny little kingdom as it is! I just want one small favor."

"What do you want?" asked Noreia. The words almost spoke themselves.

The Roc leader cackled, a sound that echoed through the hollow halls. "First, I want changing dust!"

"Absolutely not! Only the most powerful wizards can control its magic," Noreia said.

"Hostilius!" King Holocene squawked. "Where is that feather-brained attendant when I—"

"Here, Your Most Excellent Sire!" said Hostilius, flying down from the rafters.

"Bring the prisoner to me!" bellowed the Roc King.

In a minute, Noreia's father, King Roparz, was brought in. He was injured and weak. He walked with his hands tied, and his shirt was torn. His shoulder was scratched.

"You've wounded him!" cried Noreia. "I'll give you what you want!" She handed Holocene the pouch tied to her belt. Tears sparkled in her eyes.

"Now watch. You may learn something!" said the Roc King. "Darter, bring me the spell book you found from the ancient land of Lore!" His soldier brought the Roc leader a large, gilded book. Holocene opened it, turning the pages with his claw.

"You mustn't use that book," Noreia warned, trying to change his mind. "Terrible things could happen if you don't know how to cast the spells!"

"Stand back!" warned the Roc King. Then he sprinkled the changing dust over himself and spoke these words:

Shape of lion, bear, or oxen,
Undo potion, fairy toxin,
Making me another way,
Restore my human form today!

In a great eruption of black smoke, the Roc King's feathers fell away. His wings turned to human hands, and his claws turned to human feet. There stood a handsome prince in a black satin cape, velvet doublet, and black pants. He wore a short beard that he stroked vainly.

"Prince Holocene!" yelled Noreia.

"I prefer to be called *King*. I'm claiming the throne of Emerhill, Noreia!" said Holocene. "Now I will rule in place of your father. Your family is finished!" The once feathered monarch snapped his fingers and pointed to his tray for more fresh fish and cheese.

"Never!" Noreia cried out. Holocene's guards reached to take hold of her, their claws against her shoulders. Noreia struggled against them. "You will never take my father's throne!"

"Shall we lock up the princess now, Sire?" asked Hostilius.

Holocene settled comfortably back in his new throne. "Not yet. Leave me, Hostilius! I have more business to discuss with the princess at present."Noreia struggled in the grasp of the guards.

"Let her speak!" The guards let go of Noreia. "We must make a toast to my new authority," said King Holocene. "Everyone raise a glass! I am about to become King of Emerhill! Why doesn't anyone...? Well, you seem to be tied up at the present time!" He cackled ominously.

The audience of lords and ladies, attendants, and royal soldiers were tied to chairs or pillars or standing in chains. Many of them struggled against the chains to free themselves.

"All former Emerhill guards will serve me or pay for their neglect with their lives!" Then he turned to the princess.

"Your father is less steady on his feet now, Noreia. I think he seems distracted, maybe unfit to rule. I'm correct, Mother, aren't I?"

"Yes, son!" a strange woman's voice said from the back of the room. The woman's dark figure remained standing in the shadows.

"Who said that?" called Noreia. "Who is speaking from the shadows?"

An aged woman walked into the light. She wore a wreath of acanthus leaves and flowers. Her long, dark robes dragged over the floor as she reached out her arms to her son.

"Now you'll be able to rule here," she said, embracing him.

"I don't understand. What's happening? If this is your mother, how did you become—" said Noreia.

"A seabird? My mother turned me into a seabird when I was a young boy. I finally found the spell to change me back into a man," the elegant prince explained.

"I'm Prince Holocene's mother, Queen Acanthia," the elderly queen said. "Holocene is my youngest son. I changed two of my children into magical creatures. One of them lives far away, while Holocene takes care of me."

"I still don't understand. I've lived my life as a tamed seabird, due to your magical spell. Why did you turn me into a seabird, Mother?" Prince Holocene asked, his eyes frightened.

"Your father wanted to take you and your siblings away from me. He wanted adventure! Perhaps I went too far," the elderly sorceress explained. "It is good to have my son return to me again!"

"Yes, but I want something more! I want to rule Emerhill!" said Prince Holocene. "And the rest of the fairy kingdoms, as well!"

"Be cautious, my son, and wise," Queen Acanthia warned. "Not even the fairies rule over—"

"You won't get away with this, Holocene!" shouted Noreia. "My grandmother is a powerful fairy, who won't stand for your taking over the entire Fairy Realm."

"Ah ha!" said Prince Holocene. "You must know where the fairy is hiding! Better send her here or you won't get your father back."

Noreia hesitated. However, when she saw the fierce look on Holocene's face, she uttered the spell to bring the fairies.

By the sea, you live with torrents,
Wind swept waves of raging sea!
Marcelina, dear Grandmother,
Hurry now to me!

'Neath the ancient gnarled trees,
Rayenna of the land Fay Linn!
Need I now your help and magic.
Help me, friend and kin!

Flying, two are queens and fairies,
Bring ye here your wands of light,
That justice here can be!

There was a swirl of sparkling smoke that grew until it filled the room. When the smoke dispersed, Rayenna and Marcelina stood near the open window.

"Now look who we have here! Magical fairies with magical gifts!" Prince Holocene rubbed his hands together, spitting and cackling.

"Be careful what you wish for...." said Rayenna to the prince.

"You had better be cautious, or else!" said Marcelina.

"I now see the error in my ways, Holocene," said Acanthia. "No one may rule all of the Fairy Realms, for a good reason. No one could!"

"I'll just take what I want, instead! I need more changing dust. Give me that pouch you have, Marcelina!" Marcelina handed it to the prince reluctantly.

"Holocene, I beg you not to use the spell! Its magic is powerful!" said Noreia. The prince left his throne and went to a giant spell book open upon a table. The self crowned king leafed carefully through the spell book's entries. "Transformation spells with feathers, fallen leaves... changing dust! Perfect. My power will rule everyone. My true greatness will be released by the spell!"

He sprinkled the crystals from the pouch over his head and said:

> *Magic within, magic without!*
> *Magic make a turnabout!*
> *Inside nature make your way,*
> *To my outer form today!*

The book on the table of treasures quivered and shook, as if it were unsettled by the spell it was being asked to perform. A cloud of gray blue smoke seeped out of the open book. Its pages flipped in the chilly air.

Prince Holocene turned pale as his dark hair grew into pointed feathers. His fingers became claws again, and his shoulders drooped. As sparkling black smoke enveloped him, he made a strange cry, like the caw of a crow. The large crown slipped off his head and onto his shoulders.

Prince Holocene stood transformed, back into the grey-feathered Roc he had been. He looked disappointedly into a mirror.

Startled and upset by his fate, he grabbed the spell book in one claw. In the other, his talons clutched the pouch of fairy dust. He screeched to his cronies, who flew onto the shoulders of King Roparz. They grasped him and flew through the window, Noreia's father in their clutches.

Noreia gasped and screamed. She ran to the window and looked at the sea below.

Holocene swept through the sky as well. He held onto the heavy spell book with his own life in the balance. He fluttered, fighting to keep himself aloft. His grip loosened and his wings drooped, but he refused to release the book, despite its weight.

"Drop the king now!" he shouted. As Noreia watched, the Rocs let go of her father. His body was falling, closer and closer to the rocks below.

With a great flutter of his strong, heavy wings, Dormach swept through the air and saved the king from certain death.

Rocs groaned and cringed, witnessing the rescue. Noreia cheered and clapped. The king was flown to safety upon Dormach's back.

Holocene and the book fell together, freefalling from the height of the castle walls down to the water. They fell into the great ocean below the cliffs of Emerhill.

"Fogspell! Help him, please," cried Noreia.

"As you command, Noreia!" And the great General Fogspell launched himself from the windowsill. Down he flew, scooping the waterlogged Holocene from the stirring water of the great sea.

The other Rocs panicked and flew out the window after them. Countless more fluttered out from behind the castle walls in all directions, as if frightened by a strange spirit.

Rayenna said a protection spell aloud, softly.

> *Creatures of the air and ocean,*
> *Braving magic spells and potions,*
> *Let us name a rightful fairy to be queen.*

> *Though she'd never make the motion,*
> *Despite her humbleness, devotion,*
> *Noreia must be Fairy Queen!"*

The wind ceased its torment of the trees as the sound of songbirds flitted again among the branches. Ominous clouds that had roamed the pale sky unveiled the sun's warmth. The Rocs' feathered carcasses upon the cobblestones evaporated into thin air. The sky was a soft French blue again, as the gray clouds became puffy and white, gliding overhead.

Noreia found the keys that Holocene's guards had left on the table. She unlocked Emerhill people from their shackles and chains. The fairies ran from courtiers to cook to court jester, releasing them all. The elfin soldiers were given back their armor.

When the prisoners were released, they ran out to greet the welcoming sun in the courtyard. Noreia wept tears of delight as she beheld her brothers and mother walking toward her.

"Argantael! Dalwyn! You are my dearest brothers. Mother, let us embrace and forget our disagreement," said Noreia as she reached for them.

"Noreia!" Dalwyn cried, "You have saved us!" The two boys leapt to hold her in their arms.

"You rescued Father and saved the day!" shouted Argantael. "Please do not leave us. I want to know more about dragons, Noreia!"

Elves and courtiers cheered as Dormach soared into the courtyard. As Dormach flapped his wings to regain his balance, the king dismounted. There were shouts of victory as the elves worked to place a laurel wreath around the dragon's neck. A grand procession fell into line, with every fairy and sprite leading the way before the soldiers, ladies, and noblemen. They wore wreaths of flowers as they awarded the soldiers with medallions for bravery.

Dragons took to the air, breathing fireworks into the sky. A crowd of villagers, noblemen, and Emerhill guards began moving like a wave into the grand castle's throne room. Boundless was their happiness.

Noreia took her father by the hand and led him through an archway to the throne room. She kissed his cheek and bowed deeply to him. The tired king mounted the steps to his throne.

"My daughter!" said King Roparz as he opened his arms to her. "I am truly sorry for how I have treated you. You have been forthright. Dormach has demonstrated his loyalty and heroism, proving that dragons can be allied with kings."

The crowd applauded.

"Bring Holocene to me!" commanded the king. The guards brought the dripping wet creature in chains, trembling with fright.

"I believe you have my crown!" announced the king. The Roc leader reached up and brought the crown back to His Majesty.

"What will you do with me?" cried Holocene.

"You may return to the island you came from," said King Roparz.

"But I'll be alone, Your Majesty—" said Holocene.

"You are not welcome here!" the king said. "Never return here, or, if you do, I will have to punish you!"

The courtiers and soldiers burst into laughter. The

merchants chortled their deep belly laughs, while the ladies made polite chuckles. Their laughter echoed in the rafters.

The king stood to address the crowd. He nodded to Noreia, and then to Dormach, whose eyes were small enough to look through the archway from the courtyard. King Roparz cleared his throat. "Princess Noreia, please accept this small medal as a symbol of our gratitude. I give it wholeheartedly, not as your father but as your king."

Noreia stood perplexed, but she bent her head to accept the award. "Thank you, my father!" she said.

The king smiled a great smile and said these words. "Let all who live in Emerhill, or neighboring countries, behold the grand treasures I have found. My daughter, the resourceful Princess Noreia, and our brave friend Dormach, the First Dragon of Emerhill!"

THE END

ACKNOWLEDGMENTS

Thank you to my manuscript editors: Andrea Alban, A.E. Conran, and Amy Novesky. Thank you, Pamela Feinsilber and Wendy VanHatten, for your copyediting. Thank you, Deborah Kirshman, for your encouragement. Thank you, Sue Heinemann, for your insightful suggestions. Thank you, Sue Campbell, for critiquing an early manuscript for me. Thank you, Doug Childers, for help with brainstorming with me. Thank you, Autistry Studios. Thank you to Anne D. Kaiser for her management of the project and her manuscript editing and reading.

Thanks to my illustration guides and art instructors: Courtney Alexis Bell-Gimelli, Tron Bykle, Mehri Dadgar, Janet Jacobs, Suzanne Lacke, Carol Lefkowitz, and Katrina Wagner. Thank you, Dan Swearingen, for the early help with dragon models.

Thank you, Book Passage, for your classes and support. Thanks to my invaluable friends from Andrea Alban's writing critique groups. Thank you to my friends in Amy Novesky 's workshops. Thank you to Kathryn Petrocelli. Thank you, Jim Shubin, for your design expertise. Thank you, Sam Barry, for organizing the store's Path to Pub-lishing program and putting me on the path to publication of my book. Thank you, BehindTheName.com founder Mike Campbell for his permission to create many characters from historical names on the site. Thank you, Michael Chiaravalle of Brand Navigation, for your superb website design.

Thank you, Kathy Grayson Brown, for your assistance with glossary entries. My thanks to Adam, Patrick, and Danielle at Kinko's, to Bob Bennett and Jay Daniels at Black Cat Studios, and to Charli Lundholm for your help with artwork and digital photography. Thank you, Bonnie Kamin Morrissey, for your encouragement. Thank you, Dr. Marion Lane Diamond, Ph.D. and Dr. Michael Jones, Ph.D. for your foresight in diagnosing me on the spectrum. Thank you, Janet Lawson for your suggestion that I start making book illustrations. Thank you, Louise Katz. Thank you to my friends and counselors at Lifehouse. Thank you to my house manager Gary Malfatti, for helping me every day. Thanks to counselors past and present: Jodie Balter, Doug Childers, Kerry Farrell, Helen Ford, Charli Lundholm, Bonnie Kamin, Kate Kelly, Randy Kirwin, and Patricia Schermerhom.

Thank you to my physicians, especially Dr. Sajot Grewal at Tamalpais Internal Medicine, Dr. Steven Katznelson at CPMC, Dr. Scott Olson, and Dr. Adil Wakil at CPMC. Thank you to Marielena. My thanks to the CPMC transplant staff.

Thank you to my friends from Writer's Tribe®, especially Patricia Garfield, Ph.D., Rob Rosborough, Sandra Domeracki, Susan Blatty, Teri Drobnick, Gailya Magdalena Morrison, Jacquie Faber, Grace Rogers, Ph.D., Jacqueline Texier, Ann Mesritz Gronvold, Amy Torrano, Donna Hemmila, and Aidan Niles. Thank you, Nina Vincent, Vanessa Warring, Corina Winn, Geoff Wood, Diane Dalton, Ron Damberger, and Travis Darcy.

238   THE DRAGON OF EMERHILL

A special thank you to the Flickr photographers who inspired many of my illustrations. Thanks to Dominique Beau for lending me a photograph of her home in Brittany that became Marcelina's cottage. Thanks to Ben Abel for his "Ramparts Castle" photo that inspired the painting of the castle tower on page 212 A special mention to the San Francisco Botanical Gardens and Cluny Museum in Paris for inspiring me to take my own reference photos.

Thank you to the nursing staffs at Marin General Hospital, Alta Bates Hospital, CPMC, and UCSF. A special thank you to Josie at Satellite. I also need to thank my dialysis technicians and the staff at Satellite Dialysis, CPMC, and Berkeley Dialysis. To my IHSS providers, thanks for your friendship and caregiving. Thank you to Zipora Anker for your love and support. Thank you to my physicians.

Thank you to my kidney donors for giving me a life choice without dialysis. My gratitude goes to my magical godmother Pam Kramlich and to my guardian fairies Cynthia Coolidge, Piper Evans, Helen Ford, Shirley Gilbertson, Dale A. Kaiser, Charli Lundholm, Patricia Mudra, and Merry Lynn Rose.

A special thank you to my late grandfather, Dr. William F. Kaiser. I owe a great deal to my parents, Anne Kaiser and Robert Taylor, who continue to help me reach my dreams.

About the Author/Illustrator

Breton Kaiser Taylor lives in Northern California with his best friend, a toy poodle named Ginger. He began writing seriously in 2008, intending to write about his experiences with kidney failure for a teen audience. He was on dialysis life support for 20 years, and feels blessed to have received a second transplant in 2006.

Instead of writing about his medical experiences, Breton wrote and illustrated The Dragon of Emerhill, a fantasy novel for ages 8-12. The Dragon of Emerhill is the first book in a trilogy.

Breton often attends classes at Book Passage in Corte Madera and Book Passage conferences.

His poems have been published in the College of Marin Literary Magazine and he has won a poetry prize.

Kaiser Taylor also creates one of a kind jewelry, fine art illustrations for children's rooms, and pen and ink invitations.

His website is: www.thedragonofemerhill.com

Postscript

I wrote *The Dragon of Emerhill* to offer a unique and empowering fairytale. It takes place centuries ago along the bay of Emerhill Kingdom. It's an adventure of dragons making hair breadth escapes, a princess fighting for independence, and a visit to four fairy kingdoms!

Fairytales often roughly sketch roles that we ourselves are pressed to enact. Princesses often wait for their princes. In *The Dragon of Emerhill*, my heroine is both a dynamic character and an adventurous young girl. Princess Noreia has conflicting feelings about her parents. Her need for independence starts with a need to make decisions she feels are just and consistent with her beliefs.

I hope the novel's archetypal characters become more realistic and many faceted. As the story unfolds, there are guardians, fairies, monarchs, dragons, and sorcerers. Each of these characters brings to light the dilemma of understanding our fellow man. Emerhill's dragons are sympathetic and kind, which is unusual for dragons. Stalwart becomes a role model when Noreia cannot relate to her father's stoicism and warlike opinions. As her confidante and friend, this dragon is a hero to her.

The young men in the story are Prince Dalwyn and Prince Argantael, who choose divergent paths in their lives. Argantael serves as his sister's tutor by finding the knowledge she needs. Although Prince Dalwyn and Noreia follow different maps, they both share a common trait; they are both world explorers.

The story was inspired in part by Peter, Paul, and Mary's indelible song, "Puff The Magic Dragon." Stalwart does, indeed, "live by the sea" in a water cave just like Puff. In my story, the dragon's friend is a 12 year old princess. Here, Noreia must ultimately excuse herself from the comfort of childhood itself to defend her friends and their shared standards. The need to leave childhood is what sadly left Puff alone, without his friend. In Emerhill, Fairy Marcelina explains to Noreia the dilemmas of growing up.

"Every young boy loves dragons, but there is a day they all seem to find when they fear them. What we love changes, Noreia. What matters is that you care about them. "

The story takes place in the early Middle Ages in Brittany, France. Some of the kingdoms are pure fantasy. However, Brittany, Dragonera Isle, and Lismoire Isle are real places on maps of France or Majorca, Spain. The island I chose as a location, Dragonera, is the same island where J.M. Barrie was inspired to write *Peter Pan*. I didn't know this beforehand, but both stories coexist well in different centuries. In Emerhill, Dragonera is the ancient home of the royal dragons.

I have placed a story map of Emerhill and surrounding islands in the front of my book. The flora and fauna in the novel are mostly specific to Brittany and the British Isles. The themes of the book are humanity, bravery, and individuation. Noreia finds her voice of reason in both the love she has for her magical friends and her ability to establish her own part in the world.

Throughout the book, you may notice words in bold type that you can find in the glossary of my website. Some of these are medieval words, architecture terms, period costume, or actual place names. My website is available to explain your questions. Readers who want to find books I recommend, or research a subject of interest, can consult the "suggested reading" or "bibliography" sections.

The character names derive from world mythology or foreign languages. You can look for the various family trees and character names on the website, too. I hope the website will be useful. It was important to me to provide this information.

I grew up surrounded by strong and intelligent women. I wish that girls would grow up to be strong and self-assertive. They may become astronauts, professors, attorneys or physicians. Noreia is a complex character, and I hope girls can identify with her.

I hope that when boys become businessmen, soldiers, artists, or maybe scientists in their community, that they remember this novel. Perhaps they can help prevent wars with intention and discourse instead of swords. With our minds and our imaginations, we can speak out and be strong for each other. As Noreia's grandmother mentions in the story:

"— Promise me you'll never lose your curiosity
   or your hope!"

Breton Kaiser Taylor

CPSIA information can be obtained
at www.ICGtesting.com
Printed in the USA
FSHW010925151118
53770FS

9 781732 326958